THE ~~DANGER~~ LIES IN FEAR

MILTON GODFREY

APS BOOKS

APS Books

www.andrewsparke.com

APS Books is a subsidiary of the APS Publications imprint

Copyright ©2021 Milton Godfrey
All rights reserved.

Milton Godfrey has asserted his right to be identified as the author of this work in accordance with the Copyright Designs and Patents Act 1988

First published worldwide by APS Books in 2021

ISBN 978-1-78996-299-4

Dedicated to all the sufferers

CHAPTER ONE

Michael Wright fastened his seatbelt, closed his eyes and held his breath as the plane taxied along the runway at Palisados Airport. It was his first experience of a plane flight, a sensation filling him with emotions of fear, excitement and anticipation. Those feelings were to remain with him throughout the flight and long after.

As the plane became airborne, he looked through the small window next to his seat. He could see jagged rock edges along the coast fringing the blue sea below. The plane gradually gained height and headed into the distance. He tried to adjust his mind to his surroundings, while listening to the steady drone of the engines. The experience could have been a reflection of some fantasia or memory of a distant dream. There was a moment's thought about what could possibly happen in the hours ahead during flight, or in the unknown future that awaited him.

A cloud rushed by; then others in quick succession. The silvery lining of other clouds stretched far into the distance. Behind him was the glow of the setting sun. It was a situation far removed from any previous experience he had ever had.

Not so long ago he had been in the airport lounge, feeling the humidity and watching heat rise from the asphalt. He had been among crowds, hustling and bustling as they prepared for departure, while others were welcoming arrivals. Now he was high above the them all, heading into a life of uncertainty, on his way to England, with no real clarity about the future.

Any expectations he had, could have been shaped by misguided impressions from the stories told to him by those he had left behind. He had heard many such stories about what life was like abroad. Unfortunately, the people who told those stories had never travelled outside Jamaica. Most had never left their own communities or even the village where they were born. For a few, their only contact with the outside world was contained in letters from family members abroad or gleaned from listening to the radio. They had no real understanding of what the bigger world was all about. Michael treated all the stories he had heard about life abroad with scepticism. And although he didn't trust his own imagination completely, he was optimistic.

His first eleven years were spent in Jones Town and Trench Town, volatile environments. For one reason or another, those communities lived on a knife-edge of violence; fear were always close at hand. From an early age, he had learned that this was part of everyday living. Self-preservation meant learning quickly and growing up fast. Even before he had reached the age of eight, he had witnessed many quarrels, fights, knives and gun attacks. He could remember at least two occasions when his own mother had had to defend herself against vicious attacks, to preserve both their lives. Even at that young age, he couldn't understand why people treated each other with such ferocity.

Trench Town School was one of the many Michael attended. Mr Byfield, the Headmaster, and the school he ran both had a reputation for delivering good education. But it was a tough environment. Arguments, intimidation, bullying and fights among pupils, and sometimes parents in the school yard, were frequent. Later, on reflection, he had come to realise that social and economic problems, poverty, and lack of opportunity for people to escape from their predicament, were all contributory factors to the tensions and conflicts. It was survival of the fittest.

One of the first things he learned when he started school was how to survive by avoidance. Without brothers or sisters to defend him in such a tough environment, his mother taught him his first lesson:

'Head straight home after school, as fast as possible.'

His life wasn't much different from those around him. With an absent father, he was in the same predicament as many families living in those environments but his mother provided everything he needed, and he learned not to demand too much of what wasn't unavailable.

During his flight, his mind turned to the first time he met his father. He was about six years old. Although memories of that meeting were unclear, he recalled its emotions and the shedding of tears. Then his father went away and didn't return again for a number of years.

The next time he saw his father he was about nine years old.

After that they didn't meet again until four weeks before he was due to leave Jamaica for England. There were no words of explanation for the long disappearances and the only questions he might have asked weren't the kind children would ask a parents to answer. It was a very emotional final reunion. He would never see or hear from his father again, although he would try to contact him by letter from England but there would be no reply.

Michael remembered seeing his father once in the small room his mother called home. It was late at night and he was in bed pretending to be asleep when he saw his father put something on top of the wardrobe. The next morning when he was alone in the room, Michael had climbed up to see what his father had hidden secretly in the brown paper bag. He nearly fell off the chair when he saw the gun. He never mentioned it to anyone or climbed up to look on top of the wardrobe again. Afterwards he could hardly hold back the fear he felt every time he remembered that gun.

The plane was now on a steady course and the lights above the cabin door said: *UNFASTEN SEAT BELTS*. He looked around the cabin, still anxious and wishing he had reached his destination. He closed his eyes to try and sleep, but was feeling claustrophobic. It was a feeling similar to the one he had had when he was eight years old. He was playing with some boys his own age and went to look for a marble that was lost underneath a nearby house. He became tightly wedged between stilts that supported the house and the neighbours had to be called to rescue him. That sense of claustrophobia now returned to haunt him.

He had had a similar experience at the age of seven. He knew the exact date. It was August 17th, 1951 a day that had left an indelible mark. On that night Hurricane Charlie swept across the island with devastating effect, resulting in loss of both life and property. His adopted sister, Edith, who looked after him when his mother was away at work in the city, was with him. She was fourteen. That night they were alone in the small room. Their mother, Vashti, was caught downtown where she worked, selling produce from one of Michael's uncle's plantations in the country. The profits were used to buy provisions for their shop that supplied the needs of the whole district.

That hurricane would always be with him.

CHAPTER TWO

Thursday August 16th.

The radio warned of the imminent arrival of Hurricane Charlie but the news was treated casually by some with a typically easy-going Jamaican approach. Michael overheard someone remark, 'Cho, ah nuh nutten.' Another man said, 'Bwoy, storm only gwine to pass over de island, man.' A rastaman with a spliff hanging from his lips said: 'Jah will protect I an I. I man safe.'

However, even those taking a casual approach were quietly worried. They knew the devastating consequences of a direct hit on the island and prayed it wouldn't happen.

Hurricane Charlie arrived the following day as predicted.

The day began calm, sun rising with precision as usual. By midday the earth was scorched by unbearable heat. Nothing unusual about that: except in the rainy season, heat was the main feature of Jamaican weather; wall-to-wall sunshine beginning shortly after dawn.

In Kingston the hustle and bustle of daily life was in full flow, but the weather forecast was still at the fore-front of everyone's mind.

By late afternoon the sky gradually began to darken, followed by light winds and a drizzle. Everyone by then was making preparations to board up their windows. There was a rising sense of urgency, as if they had all suddenly remembered the details of the previous day's broadcast. News on the local radio was now announcing the imminent arrival of Hurricane Charlie.

Most people were, of course, accustomed to following emergency routines over the years, during hurricane season. It was part of everyday life in the Caribbean but Michael had never had that experience before. When he saw people boarding up their windows, he realised that something he had never seen was about to happen. The other children around him also watched with excitement but the danger soon became obvious. Much darker clouds were approaching, darkening the sky. Wind and rain gathered pace and everyone started to head for the safety of their own small houses or to the rooms they called home.

Unlike Michael Edith had experienced at least two minor hurricanes but they had caused very little damage or trauma so even she was unprepared for the severity of what happened next and the people living in the adjoining yards were too busy preparing for the hurricane to notice that Michael and his adopted sister were home alone and Edith hadn't cottoned on to the urgent need to get Michael indoors. Indeed, he and two boys about the same age, were still playing in the middle of the community yard, amid the drizzle and progressively darkening sky, having fun, while darkening clouds were gathering quickly with each passing moment.

When Edith finally called out to him, Michael ran towards the room they called home and Edith bolted the door as soon as Michael was inside.

Within an hour, wind was howling, the rain was torrential and mass lightening flashed. Peels of thunder were constantly crashing down. By now, most who had been busy preparing for the hurricane were in a place of safety, hoping and praying that the storm would pass quickly.

Michael had seen some heavy rains before. He could remember seeing floods threaten to wash away everything in its path and the gully that ran along Central Road had carried fast flowing flood waters towards the sea. He had heard talk of how treacherous the torrents rushing along the gully could be and had been warned by his mother more times than he could remember. Whenever he gazed at the rushing water he would always remind himself to keep a safe distance. He had heard stories of children and adults who had fallen in the gully and been swept away to the sea half a mile away from his home. Whether those stories were true or made up to create a climate of fear in his mind, to him they were real. The image of the water rushing towards the sea was the first picture that came to his mind now as soon as the rain began to beat strongly down onto the corrugated roof of the small room where they had locked themselves away. He longed for the warm of his mother and her comforting voice to reassure him.

The wind gathered pace. It seemed to be increasing with every passing moment. As the hurricane started to batter their small room, Michael felt a sense of isolation, of helplessness. He and Edith both resigned themselves to the idea that no one was on the way to rescue or comfort them.

The hurricane at its most intense sounded as if at any moment the roof would be torn off, exposing them to the elements that were trying to invade the room. They hid beneath the confined space of the bed and huddled together. Wind and rain lashed the room with ferocity and the sound of thunderclaps echoed through the darkness of the night. They could hear trees and debris crashing down as the raging winds howled like a demon in a blackness outside lit up only by the lightning strikes. Corrugated irons crashed against the side of the room and nearby houses. The light bulb in the room exploded and they were in complete darkness, without even a torch or candle. Water began pouring in from a hole in the roof and crevices of the window that faced east.

After more than an hour, there was a brief moment of respite, a moment that lasted several minutes. That moment gave them hope that the storm was passing but that was wishful thinking. Before long the surges increased once more; this time even with more intensity. The noise became unbearable. Their clothes were now soaking wet and so was everything else in the room, except perhaps the clothes in the locked wardrobe.

Several hours passed but the hurricane was still raging. They lost track of time and were now weak from fear and becoming traumatised - tears mixed with rain water streamed down their faces.

In the midst of the cacophony of noise and deluge, they thought they could hear voices calling out. The voices, mingled with the howling wind, rain, lightning and thunder, seemed distantly eerie. They weren't sure if they were imagining things but stopped sobbing to listen.

Someone began pounding the door of their room, and a number of frantic voices were calling out for help amidst the pounding. The desperate sounding voices and banging on the door startled them, but were welcome signs of life outside. They got out from beneath the bed and tried to open the door, but the wind threatened to tear it from its hinges and pin them to the wall. Using all their strength, they managed to unbolt the door and three adults, two men and a woman, collapsed across the threshold into the room. They were total strangers but, for Michael and Edith, a welcome sight. They weren't alone any more.

It was a fierce struggle to close the door. The newcomers were mumbling and sobbing through wet and trembling lips but eventually managed to get the bolt back in place.

Surprised to see two children alone and in a state of panic, the woman tried to comfort Michael who was now crying uncontrollably and then opened the wardrobe to look for dry clothes in the darkness of the room. The hole in the roof was now much bigger and wind and rain was increasingly invading the room but she found and put an oversized shirt on Michael.

The men chattered frantically as they tried to figure out what to do next. There were more tears, sobbing and prayers as if they felt these were their last moments. The adults were asking God to have mercy on their souls but all such requests for mercy fell on deaf ears as the wind howled. The sound of thunder echoed through the night as it seemingly crashed against the sides of the small room. One of the men shouted 'We're all going to die', adding yet more anxiety to an already distressing situation.

Michael started to think about heaven. The mission church he went to on Sunday mornings had taught him that all good children go to heaven. He couldn't remember anything bad he had done that would prevent him going to heaven and that gave him some sense of security. But although he wanted to go to heaven, he wanted to get there without dying. He was saying the Lord's Prayer silently, sobbing, hoping to be rescued from the dangers of the night.

There was another urgent hammering at the door, about ten minutes after the three strangers first arrived, accompanied by a desperate cry for help. The adults levered open the door, again struggling against the wind and rain. A man staggered in with a bag of mangoes over his shoulders and fell to the floor, exhausted. He was helped to his feet and recognised by the men who helped him up. They lived near each other, but the hurricane had also destroyed his house.

Recovering a little the newcomer opened his bag and handed everyone a mango, which by this time was beyond welcome. Michael hadn't eaten for several hours. Fear and trauma had destroyed his desire for food. But the offer of a mango, now that there was an element of security with adults around, was like being invited to a feast. Everyone in their soaking wet clothes and trembling lips devoured the mangoes but their moment of respite from hunger was suddenly interrupted. The window flew open and everyone screamed as wind and rain invaded the room.

The men struggled to close it again. There were more desperate gasps and sighs.

The man with the bag of mangoes shouted, 'The roof's gone, the roof's gone!'

He meant the roof of a house he could see through the window. but everyone else thought he was talking about the roof of the room they were in and they all rushed out into the dangers of the night, amidst roaring winds and flying debris.

Michael and Edith followed, hanging onto the woman's dress.

They struggled through the darkness, unsure of where to go. Lightning flashed and high winds buffeted them as they were tossed from side to side. There was a house about fifty yards away and they headed in that direction half paddling through water, . They fell several times as they bobbed and weaved to avoid litter on the ground and flying object coming from all directions.

The house they were heading for belonged to a local landlord, Mr Palmer. It was one of the biggest and most secure houses in the neighbourhood but the front door was wide open. The house was in darkness and water, broken crockery and furniture littered the floor. The windows had been blown open and the shutters were banging from side to side. There was no one home. The men tried to close the windows but failed dismally. Without any spoken agreement they all headed for another nearby shelter, a house on stilts, not too far away.

Many such houses were built on stilts to avoid flooding but houses on stilts also served another purpose. They were convenient, if anyone wanted to move their home on a truck or trailer, to a new location.

This house, on a slight slope, was on very high stilts and was in total darkness. They could hear the sound of things being thrown around inside the house in the furore. They ran for shelter beneath the house. Even though the water beneath the house was flowing fast it was safer than being outdoors. Everyone desperately clung to the stilts supporting the house and argued about what to do next causing more confusion and anxiety.

Before long there was another surge of wind and rain and in less than five minutes the water beneath the house became extremely treacherous. The oversized shirt Michael was wearing was torn from his body and he screamed as water threatened to overpower him and loosen the grip he had on the stilt. He held on with one hand and with the other clung to the woman's arm. It was a daunting task for a seven year old and he could feel his strength ebbing away. He braced himself against one of the stilts, sobbing, shaking with fear and the cold.

It was a desperate situation and even the adults seemed to be now concerned with their own survival. Someone shouted that the house might collapse on them. In the chaos and confusion, another torrent of water washed them from beneath the house and they were once more exposed to the elements. At first they were able to cling to each other but they soon everyone was washed in different directions and Michael and Edith were separated from the adults. They just about managed to cling on to each other as the flood water carried them in the direction of Miss Dolly's house.

Miss Dolly was a middle-aged woman. Her husband kept goats and they were well off by Trench Town standards. She was Aunt Dolly to all the children in the neighbourhood. Sometimes children would meet in her yard to play because she was tolerant. Her house was a kind of unspoken neighbourhood crèche and people would sometimes leave their children in her trust, if they had important things to do. If she had known that Michael and Edith were alone, marooned by the storm, she would have been the first to attempt to rescue them. Her house was large enough to accommodate many people, if she had to. And even though she was a well-off member of the community, she didn't have an attitude problem. She treated everyone in the neighbourhood with equal courtesy and respect. So she was well protected, safe in an environment where, if you had too much of anything and were arrogant about it, there would always be a lot of people trying to relieve you of some of it and they would do it one way or another. Miss Dolly didn't have those concerns.

Her house, also on stilts, was somewhat sheltered, and a little way from the mainstream of flood waters. Beneath it was a refuge for goats her husband kept. Goats didn't like rainy seasons either, so her house on stilts was an ideal place for them to shelter when it rained. That was the place Michael and Edith crawled into as soon as they reached the house. They crawled between the goats to get warm and regain their strength.

It was some time before they ventured out into the open again to knock the front door for the first time but they didn't even have the strength to cry or shout anymore. Buffeted by wind and rain, they banged on the door with all their might but all their efforts to be heard were muted by the storm.

They retreated to safety beneath the house again. With their strength ebbing away, they decided they had to make one final effort before resigning themselves to the likelihood that they would not survive the night. The goats were silent, as if they too had resigned to their fate. The moment of despair had arrived and in one last desperate attempt, they crawled from beneath the house and pounded the door with all their might before collapsing in the midst of the wind and rain in front of the stubbornly sealed door.

The hours of their ordeal had sapped all their strength and they were now merely surviving by willpower alone. They were in danger of drowning, of dying from hypothermia, or of being fatally injured by flying debris.

Almost on the verge of being unconscious, they heard the sound of the door being opened and they were plucked from the darkness and devastation by Miss Dolly's husband and carried into the safety of the house. By instinct, or an act of God, he had thought he could hear the faint voices of children calling out. He hadn't been quite sure whether it was his imagination or the children in the back room having nightmares but his check outside had saved two lives that were facing almost certain death.

Miss Dolly quickly wrapped Michael, who was naked, in a large towel and removed Edith's wet clothes. They were both rigorously rubbed down with a good helping of bay rum, bundled into oversized but dry clothes, and given a warm drink of chocolate tea and some hard dough bread, still trembling and sobbing while they ate.

They were later put in one of the double beds among other children who were fast asleep. The last thing Michael could remember was Miss Dolly sitting in a rocking chair, rocking, humming some improvised lullaby and watching them as they fell asleep.

The next morning, Michael opened his eyes and realised he was in a bed filled with children of all ages, some from other neighbourhoods. For him, the night's events were almost like a dream. The hurricane was over and there was an unusual calm, as if nothing unusual had happened the previous night.

Miss Dolly fed everyone before they went outdoors to see the devastation. The sun was intense and by late afternoon a lot of the rainwater quickly evaporated, bringing back a semblance of normality. People were trying to salvage something from the nothing they had had before. Children played with broken twigs and strange bits and pieces found in tangled heaps in the middle of the community yard. They were reunited with parents; everyone cried with joy to see loved ones again and it wasn't long before Michael was reunited with his mother. She had spent the night in Coronation Market where she was caught up in the storm. Her eyes were swollen from crying all night, worried about the safety of her children. She was overcome with emotion as she embraced them, thanking Miss Dolly for rescuing them from the storm.

That hurricane experience was still vivid in Michael's mind, even in the midst of his maiden flight. It was as if it happened yesterday.

Just then the plane went through an air pocket and shuddered. He closed his eyes, not wanting to think of the inevitable if something went seriously wrong. He drifted off to sleep as the plane continued without any further hint of turbulence.

'Would you like something to eat, sir?' said the stewardess, tapping him on the shoulder. The voice seemed distant, mysterious.

He opened his eyes as he turned to face the stewardess.

She handed him a menu and he searched for something unusual to eat finally ordering cream of asparagus soup, the best of everything available and went back to sleep. He still felt uncomfortable flying and didn't really want to stay awake. He wasn't afraid of dying, but had made up his mind that, if there was going to be a fatal accident, he didn't want to know about it.

Throughout the flight that became his routine. He would eat, go back to sleep and wake again when it was time to eat and the stewardess only woke him for the last time to get him to fasten his seat belt and prepare for landing.

CHAPTER THREE

The plane landed in a mist engulfing the whole airport.

A sudden gust of wind penetrated the tropical suit Michael was wearing. He felt like a visitor from another planet trying to come to terms with being hurled into another dimension where people, time, space, and the weather all needed decoding. He was in the midst of a cacophony of sounds, activities and people, all very different from those he had left behind. But he had his instructions written down long before he left Jamaica and knew exactly what to do. As soon as his luggage and passport were cleared, he got into a taxi and headed for his destination.

Looking out at London through the windows of a black taxicab he could have been a story he had read a long time ago. London traffic, fog, the London lights, delicatessen shops, the smell of fish and chips, the odour of the Thames itself, all heightened his senses. People were snuggled into warm overcoats, going about in haste to escape the chill. Red buses, more black cabs, the noise of trains, all filled him with curiosity and excitement. He tried to internalise everything he could see, hear and imagine. But all that was eventually pushed to the back of his mind as he focused on reaching his destination.

They drove through London in silence, the taxi driver barely participating in any meaningful conversation. That gave Michael time to consider and deal with all the uncertainty of arriving in a foreign land. They reached Paddington and he paid off the taxi driver. He just wanted to reach his destination as soon as possible and escape the biting wind.

As he got out of the taxi, he tried to familiarise himself with his brick and concrete surroundings and the strange looking houses with smoke coming from their chimneys. Walking along the one-way street, staring eyes made him feel uncomfortably out of place but he walked on, trying to pretend he was not the total stranger he was. He turned the corner and quickened his steps, looking at the number on each door as he passed.

Soon he was standing looking up at a tall building. The front door was ajar and he walked inside finding his feet upon a piece of worn out carpet. As he looked around, now certainly behaving like a stranger unsure what to do next, he could hear voices upstairs. He listened then walked towards the dimly lit staircase where he thought the voices were coming from. He stopped again and listened, but there was silence. He began climbing the stairs, dragging his suitcase behind him, hoping to find someone to talk to. He reached another landing and stopped for a moment to catch his breath. The weighty suitcase, loaded with food and rum for his uncle, was beginning to take its toll on his already jet-logged-body.

He decided to turn right and continue along the landing. He could now plainly make out two people talking and laughing but still wasn't sure where the voices were coming from. He had the feeling someone was watching him secretly from some obscured corner of the house.

There were more small stairs leading to another landing. As he climbed it he could see the barely visible face of a man peeping from behind a door. As he got close to the door, it slammed shut.

Just then he heard footsteps and looking down saw the woman climbing the stairs. He instantly knew she was the landlady. Her face was fixed in an angry expression. Her body language displayed a brashness that said she was not the kind of person to compromise or negotiate. Even from a distance, he imagined her to be someone who would thrive on conflict, ready for verbal confrontation at a moment's notice. She stared at him as she climbed the stairs and he stood and waited in anticipation, not sure what to say, or what might happen next.

As she came closer, he glanced at her hairstyle. It was an old fashioned perm that looked like a bird's nest. It complemented the look on her face. Her dress wasn't the latest fashion from Paris either. It was long, black, covering the top of her *granny-shoes*. She had on a red apron that seemed the perfect match for her persona and she passed him without even saying hello, gesticulating with her head for him to follow. She was obviously expecting him.

He followed her without saying a word.

Dangling the bunch of keys in her hand, she would glance behind to check he was still behind her. They climbed another small flight of stairs that led to an attic room. She stopped abruptly outside the door, opened it, and then gave him a key.

'Ee'yu'r,' she said, nonchalant. 'This is where yu'r staying. Yu'r uncle's paid you rent. Ah don't want any drunks eer. If you get drunk or sick on de floor, or break any rules, ah should call de pleece. Ah don't want no prostitute eer either. Me name's Agnes.'

He told her his name and she acknowledged by nodding her head as she walked away.

He dragged his suitcase into the room and sat on the edge of the bed. Exhausted from tiredness and fatigue, he felt tense, unwelcome. More than five thousand miles from home, he couldn't understand the absence of that fine English hospitality he had been told to expect when he arrived in England. *Maybe she's had a bad day*, he thought. Come to think of it, the airport officials who checked his luggage and passport hadn't seemed all that friendly either. Nor the taxi driver. He was beginning to think maybe they had all had a bad day.

For a moment, he thought about trying to find Agnes again to tell her that he had never slept with a prostitute. In fact, he had never slept with a woman of any kind, or tasted alcohol but reason told him to keep his emotions and flippant thoughts to himself. He suddenly remembered that he was in a foreign country. He hadn't even seen his uncle yet, so it wasn't time to be witty. He was sure his uncle would be coming before very long. His uncle surely knew he would be arriving with rum from Jamaica, a good enough incentive to come and see him as soon as possible. He sat on the edge of the bed, feeling too exhausted to even take off his crumpled suit.

The attic room was cold, damp, and the wallpaper beside the bed was beginning to peel away. The windows rattled with the slightest gust of wind and noise and the vibrations from passing trains were loud, continuous. He tried to unwind but couldn't. He took off his clothes, climbed into bed and lay facing the window that overlooked the busy railway station. Feeling worn out and isolated, the only destination now on his mind was sleep. He could hear noisy laughter downstairs and passing trains shattered the occasional silence but nothing could prevent him sleeping.

The noise of a passing train combined with a muffled knock on his room door disturbed his sleep and interrupted what seemed a lucid dream. The door was pushed open and Agnes walked in.

'Cuppa for you,' she said in a blandly unemotional voice. She put the cup of tea on the dressing table and left immediately without saying another word, closing the door loudly behind her. His watch had stopped and he couldn't imagine what time it was. He tasted the sugarless tea, put it back on the dressing table and looked out of the window. He could barely see anything through the fog. There was the noise of traffic and footsteps going about in a hurry. He imagined it was morning, but didn't understand why he couldn't see the sun.

Vague memories of his interrupted dream pieced themselves together as he looked out of the window.

He could remember running on a railway line, inside a tunnel. The train was behind him. He had started running faster, but no matter how fast he ran, the tunnel exit seemed farther away. The train eventually caught up and knocked him over onto the track but safely passed over him. It took a long time and he could remember gasping for breath and praying for the last coach to pass. He got up and started running after the train. It slowed down; he caught it and clambered aboard. The carriage was crowded and although almost out of breath, he tried not to look conspicuous. There was a conductor shouting: 'Tickets please, tickets please.' He kept repeating the same thing over and over. He approached Michael and asked him for his ticket. He started to search his pockets but couldn't find it. He just shook his shoulders and played at absent mindedness. He couldn't remember buying a ticket, why he was on the train, or where he was going. The conductor left, promising he'd be back later. The train slowed down. Up ahead was an old, dilapidated house with tinted windows. The train stopped and passengers got off and walked towards the house. Michael followed them from a little distance, curious to see what was in the house. He heard the voice of the conductor again, asking for tickets.

It was then that the noise of the train became his landlady's knock on the attic room door and his dream had rolled away.

It didn't take him long to dismiss the dream as an insignificant, response to the sounds of passing trains. He realised it must be approaching midday and he started to unpack his suitcase.

There was a knock at his door and he opened it to see the unshaven face of his Uncle Ben. He felt a sense of relief at his uncle's wide smile. Before long they were deep into conversation about what was happening in Jamaica and then of course, the question of rum surfaced. When Michael told him he had brought four bottles, his uncle's eyes lit up and his bearded smile became more pronounced.

Michael passed over the bottles along with letters, messages and gifts sent by family and friends. Uncle Ben put them in a bag and left after about an hour. He said he had some business to take care of and would be back later. Michael knew that later, by Jamaican punctuality standards, could mean the next few hours, a couple of days, or even a week. He got dressed and waited, hoping that he wouldn't get another visit from Agnes.

Uncle Ben returned several hours later with two friends and the smell of white rum on his breath.

Along with Michael, they headed for Brixton to meet some more friends.

Uncle Ben's real name was Benjamin Marcellus King and he had a passion for playing dominoes, the national pastime before he left Jamaica. It was a passion he brought with him to England, as did so many West Indian men. Several of such men sat around a large, round, domino table. Michael was briefly introduced to them and to four other men at a smaller table in mid-game.

The conversation began with talk about the good old days in Jamaica. The presence of white run, directly from Jamaica could not do other than bring out the best humour and Uncle Ben was soon toasting all kinds of occasion, many of them trivial, just an excuse to pour another drink. Michael already knew Uncle Ben's history as a heavy drinker could be traced all the way back to Jamaica. He was knew of his reputation as a womaniser, one of the main reasons why his wife divorced him and went to live in America.

Uncle Ben stood up, taking centre stage, beginning one of his famously colourful stories. 'In Jamaica we have some dangerous men. Back home, a man could kill you instantly by just one look. You believe me, Sweet Man?'

'Yes, sure.' said Sweet Man, laughing loudly.

'Still,' continued Uncle Ben, 'if you sharpen you machete and give them one raas chop, it's all over. Dead! Just like anybody else. Some man is thief as well. They would thief you goat, kill it, sell you the meat and you wouldn't know the difference.'

'You mean to say them kinda man is butcher as well?' said Manto, raising his glass and draining it.

There was silence. Even the domino players stopped playing. They were anticipating verbal banter and they didn't have to wait long. Uncle Ben stared hard at Manto. No-one, even the domino players know exactly what to expect. They waited Uncle Ben's response with bated breath.

'How you so foolish, bwoy? Weh you born, Inglan or Jamaica? Why you have to try and twiss up everything people say?' He reached for the bottle of white rum as soon as he finished the sentence, as if to call time out. He poured himself a drink and made another obscure toast.

Manto was the type of man who could easily become a victim of good humour, especially when men were playing dominoes and drinking white rum. He wasn't exactly regarded as a village idiot, or treated that way but often set himself up as a victim by interrupting Uncle Ben's conversation at the wrong time. Michael wasn't sure if Manto was deliberately trying to be a devil's advocate. That was the impression Manto gave him. It seemed to him that Manto was the sort of man who would be among the first to join in any laughter, even if someone was making fun of him.

At times he might laugh without being quite sure why he was laughing. Through an earlier digression in the conversation, Michael had already learned that Manto's wife had also left him, and it wasn't difficult to understand why.

Uncle Ben took a large sip of rum from his glass and continued where he left off. 'I hear that when Manto was in Jamaica, he wasn't afraid of anybody.'

'Is it true you nearly kill a duppy when you was back home, Uncle Ben? You know, a ghost…' said Manto, trying to win the word-play.

Mildly agitated, Uncle Ben was quick to react. 'Why don't you all keep that bwoy quiet so I can finish talking? And don't give him no more rum because his head isn't too good. Tell him to shut up, Sweet Man.'

'Manto,' said Sweet Man, half-heartedly, trying with great difficulty to disguise laughter. 'Uncle Ben say to shut up.'

Manto shuffled on his chair, folding his arms, as if he had lost interest. He was quiet for a moment, then said: 'If you say so, Sweet Man, if you say so. You know I respect your opinion.'

Sweet Man's opinion was obviously well respected, in times of good or ill humour. He had a way of using diplomacy to pacify things, without taking sides. To Michael he seemed the type to prolong humour and suspense with his coyness. Throughout the evening he had acted as a kind of arbitrator between the men sitting by the round table, and those playing dominoes. Even Uncle Ben seemed to respect his opinions given in jest as they were.

Domino playing is similar to being in a barber shop. It invites all kinds of conversation. Whatever wide and varied subjects men might talk about in the absence of women. Michael had never been in such exclusively masculine company and he was surprised to hear some of the things that came out in the almost idle talk. He listened, saying very little, except when invited to give an opinion. The first rum bottle was almost empty, the domino players were disputing previous games and the good humour continued to prevail even as the rum was taking effect, but Uncle Ben would not be outdone. He had worked in America on farm contracts, like many other Jamaicans through the nineteen fifties and sixties. He had spent time in Cuba and Panama and knew many weird and wonderful stories which he was only too frequently disposed to wheel out for an audience.. Needless to say, many were rose-coloured to say the very least.

Michael could remember the first time he ever met his uncle returning from a last trip to America with a pseudo American accent and a charismatic way with him. Well dressed and flamboyant, he was liked by nearly everyone, especially women, because he had travelled. He was Michael's mother's elder brother and he had helped her to get all the necessary documents to travel to Canada, where she was even now working to finance Michael's education.

Ben took control of the conversation again, focussing all his attention on Manto. He was now more animated, gesticulating with his hands, obviously inspired by Mr. J Wray and Nephew's white rum. 'People like you don't know anything about life,' he said, pointing at Manto. 'My granddaddy used to say that you can't learn anything until you start to live. And you don't start living yet, or know anything about life. My granddaddy used to tell me about a man called Dr Kitch who had a three-legged monkey. Sometimes the monkey would smoke a ganja pipe and chat foreign language. People would come from miles around to see this monkey.

'Of course they had to give the monkey's owner a little change.

Business as usual. But as soon as the monkey got high and start to carry on with his antics, people would cuss raas and run. They weren't sure whether the monkey would attack them.'

'You believe all them things, Sweet Man? Monkey can't talk!' said Manto, reaching for his glass, now almost empty.

'Well,' said Sweet Man, choking behind laughter. 'I don't really have any reason to disbelieve Uncle Ben, right now.'

'Suppose his granddaddy was drinking rum when he tell him that story?' yelled Manto, looking Sweet Man straight in the eye.

Sweet Man, now poker-faced and wide eyed, remained silent, as if to imply, the ball was now in somebody else's court.

Manto nearly fell off his chair as the combination of laughter and white rum began to do their job of subduing at least one victim. There was more raucous laughter as Manto was rescued from his embarrassment by Michael and Linton who caught his chair in time, just before it toppled.

'Well my granddaddy didn't drink rum,' said Uncle Ben, annoyed at being interrupted again by Manto's antics. 'But you see, Dr Kitch was a good-looking Syrian man and he had plenty women. He would tell them that ghosts were following them, then give them a silver chain with a cross to wear around their neck; then try to seduce them. Some people even say he had a son in my district.'

'Who?' interrupted Manto, leaning forward to listen more closely, eyes wide open.

'Well it sure as hell wasn't you. You're too raas ugly.' Uncle Ben's face registered his laughter. 'And I wouldn't tell you even if I know. I don't want you to call my name to anybody and say that I say. According to my granddaddy, when Dr. Kitch was around, there was plenty ghost and plenty women.'

'You know…' said Manto.

Before he could continue, Uncle Ben interrupted him; 'We know you is a big time brain surgeon, but we don't want to know because you're drunk.'

They were swamped by more loud laughter.

Linton Douglas was sitting close to Michael, enjoying the humour and sharing in the laughter but not the conversation. It was a typical scenario when boys were in the company of older West Indian men. It felt a privilege to be listening to and learning from older men's experience and hearing their outrageous stories. Michael and Linton had a lot in common. Nearly the same age, they had both come to England to study, Linton to study medicine and Michael to study law.

It was the perception of reality for most West Indian parents then that a good education would transcend all barriers and they all wanted their children to be lawyers, doctors or teachers as an escape route from the poverty and cruelty of the years of slavery and colonialism. Those generational memories became the driving force for future generations. No doubt their forebears had made them only too aware that during the centuries of enslavement, slaves weren't permitted to learn to read and write. Most believed then, and many still do, that education and submission to religion and the church was, and is, the path to liberation. Some believed that it was the will of God that people were in such a predicament and that education and religion would free them. It was a pity that they missed the part of the historical script where Christianity and the church were in favour of slavery and profited from it. Unfortunately, many still believed that heaven would receive them with open arms, if they turned the other cheek. They were conditioned to accept and endure the hardships of life, the inequities, and racism. It was a price paid for the condition of being black.

As Sweet Man pointed out in the ongoing conversation: 'They don't realise how divisive Western Christianity have been, in subduing the mind and suppressing thinking. It locks you into a program from which it is hard to escape. The second part of the script about education that nearly everyone missed is that, there is a cut-off point, in terms of the progress you are allowed to make. That's the nature of the system.'

Sweet Man's sayings tallied firmly with Michael's opinions and he didn't doubt that he would have substantial issues ahead of him to overcome.

Uncle Ben was now talking passionately about Jamaica. After living in England for six years, going back home penniless would be a tragedy. He was like a man whose dreams had been shattered by one thing or another, over the years. Alcohol, late nights, womanising, factory work, had all contributed to putting the finishing touches to his hope of recapturing something of his adventurous past.

It wasn't the way Michael remembered him from years before. The image he had held in his mind bore no resemblance to the man before him who was now bordering on melancholia, trying to mask that trait with alcohol, laughter and reminisces. The strong, energetic man who had been Michael's hero, now seemed a shadow of the past.

Michael was compassionate though. He realised that in Ben he was looking at a man who had travelled and done it all, gaining a variety of experiences and knowledge and earning the right to live his life however he thought fit, especially if his somewhat chequered life made him happy.

For Michael, meeting his Uncle again, however diminished, was a good experience, and getting to know Sweet Man, who might become a friend, even a best friend, was a fine thing. He learned that Sweet Man had spent nearly the same length of time in England as Uncle Ben and that his real name was Donald Perkins. He was an economics graduate now reduced to working in a factory. He was clearly disappointed that England had nothing better to offer him, despite his education but seemed philosophical about his fortunes.

It was Sweet Man who now reminded everyone that Michael was a new arrival in England. He knocked the bottom of his glass on the table to get everyone's attention. 'It's strange how this young man come all the way from Jamaica and Uncle Ben didn't even introduce him properly. What kinda business that, Uncle Ben?'

'Game block, six count,' shouted one of the domino players.

'Pack up the domino playing now, man. Uncle Ben have something to say,' continued Sweet Man, this time in a louder tone of voice that demanded attention.

The domino players put down their pieces to listen and Uncle Ben stood up, expanded his chest and drained his glass. 'This is my nephew, Michael, and he's the one who supplied the fire water.' He took up the bottle to pour a drink but found the bottle was nearly empty. 'Manto, since you make so much trouble all night, you can go upstairs and bring a new bottle of rum in the wardrobe. Man can't toast with empty glass.'

He didn't have to repeat himself. Manto, who by now had recovered somewhat from the effects of his earlier inebriation, licked his lips and without hesitation, charged upstairs for more rum.

Glasses were then filled and raised at Uncle Ben's command. He continued: 'I'm not going to make no long speech. All I have to say is this…this is my nephew, Michael. He's a good boy, so look after him and show him the ropes. His mother is in Canada and he's here to study law, so help him steer clear of pressure.'

'Big time Barrister, eh?' shouted someone from across the domino table.

'Remember the name, Michael Wright. Let's drink to Michael.'

Everyone took swigs from their glasses and expressed a collective wish for Michael to tell them what was happening in Jamaica. He didn't have a lot to say but telling them his experiences made him immediately homesick.

The end of the dominoes opened the way to more serious conversations and then to politics.

This was one of Sweet Man's favourite topics and he didn't hesitate. 'Michael and Linton, because you two just come to England, you might not want to hear talk about politics. But we have to face reality. That's what life is all about. The same way we have right and wrong, good and evil, large and small, in England we have black people and white people and politics. And we can't deny that we're different. Why shouldn't we be? After all, variety is the spice of life. That's exactly why we have politics, because people have different taste, culture, and different opinions.

'In England, some people go out of their way to make sure they let you know that you're different and most times your opinion doesn't count. Well, it counts, if you vote, but that doesn't say anything will change. They might not tell you directly, but you'll soon know by their actions, body language and sometimes what they say to you. Of course, not everybody is like that. There are always exceptions to the rule. There are lots of kind, loving and good people among the bad ones.'

Michael acknowledged Sweet Man, nodding his head to show his undivided attention. He didn't know much about politics in England, Jamaica, or anywhere else, but was certainly beginning to respect Sweet Man's opinion and that some of what Sweet Man was saying must have substance.

Sweet Man went on to talk about black people in European societies, historical events and how these events affect black people all over the world. He touched at length on how West Indians were invited to England to help rebuild Post War Britain and that although many West Indians were paid less for doing some of the worst jobs, it was a better opportunity than most had had back in the Caribbean.

Everyone was now entranced, listening without interruption, and occasionally sipping their rum.

Sweet Man then referred to *The Empire Windrush*, a former German Pleasure Cruiser seized during World War Two which landed the first batch of West Indians to England, mainly Jamaicans, at Tilbury Docks in 1948. Most were former soldiers who had served with Britain in the war. Nobody other than Sweet Man and Uncle Ben seemed to know this already.

As far as Michael was concerned he was learning an important piece of Caribbean history.

Sweet Man said he believed in the long run, West Indians and their offspring in England would end up on the fringe of British society because of social, economic, political decisions, and amendment to Immigration Laws. He didn't give any details. He just said: 'If you don't believe me, wait and see.'

Michael had had no idea before that night that people in England were denied opportunities because of their skin colour. He didn't even know that colour was a political issue in the minds of people.

'We're here,' said Sweet Man, 'because of the great conspiracy which began in the fifteenth century. European imperial powers decided to colonise and enslave others for economic benefits. Francis Drake, John Hawkins, Walter Raleigh – all English Pirates - all participants. That's why we are here. The Bible and the gun were kept everyone subdued, in check. Now-a-days, the conspiracy and collaboration is dressed up to look different. Institutional racism, prejudice, nationalism, patriotism, exploitation, lies, deception, are all insidious. These are all bedded into the system to satisfy the needs of the system. The system can only survive through a certain amount of exploitation. That's the nature of a capitalist society.

'Even poor working class white people in this country suffer the consequences of being poor and under-privileged. Sometimes institutions and the status quo frustrate your efforts, by keep reminding you who you are and where they think you belong socially and economically; not by word, but through stealth. The truth is, before you're born, everyone is ascribed a social and economic position. The worse thing is, people try to protect the truth by denying that these under cover activities exist. If you challenge the status quo about your rights as a black person you get a criminal record. If you persist, you're likely to end up in a psychiatric ward or neutralised, somehow. And you know what it looks like to me?'

Sweet man paused and took a large sip of rum.

'I think that nearly everyone wearing uniform and the institutions they belong to, are from the same school of thought. They're all cooking the same pot, quietly, because they think they have a divine right to do as they please. They know they can get away with it because the law machine doesn't strike a fair balance when applying the rule of law. But one day when some of our balls are hanging from Nelson's Column, in Trafalgar Square, we'll wake up and realise the truth. Things might change but they aren't changing yet, and they won't change by themselves, or maybe never.'

The conversation had turned into an impromptu lecture which not even Uncle Ben had interrupted. Now as the talking continued into the small hours of the morning, the second rum bottle was almost empty and alcohol and tiredness were getting the better of everyone, except Michael and Linton who had nothing to drink even though they had been repeatedly offered glasses. One of the domino players nearly fell off his chair and another started snoring. A long night of reminiscing, drinking, domino playing, humour, discussions, arguments, excitement, and political talk, was at an end.

Uncle Ben it seemed had a rented room in a house shared by four other men but he decided to travel home with Michael in a taxi dropping the broadest of hints that he would be staying overnight. Michael strongly suspected that Agnes was probably Ben's lover .

His suspicions were justified. They arrived home, Uncle Ben staggered from the taxi into the hall way, said goodnight and staggered towards Agnes's room.

Michael went to the sanctuary of his own attic room.

CHAPTER FOUR

Heavy snow fell all day, camouflaging rooftops and breaking the outline of houses and factories. Within those buildings, the rhythms of beating hearts of people and manufacturing machinery were active. Outdoors, wind whistled, forcing its way through the crevices of Michael's attic room windows, dampening his enthusiasm for outdoor life. It was his first experience of snow and from his window he could see slow moving traffic and people hurrying back and forth. He tried to imagine what it was like to be outdoors. He could see slumped shoulders and bowed heads, hurrying to and from their destinations. No doubt some were wishing they were somewhere else, rather than competing with the elements of nature. The groaning noise of slow moving traffic and passing trains seemed to complement the moment, as if they too felt the burden of a winter's day in England.

It was a complete contrast to anything Michael had experienced in Jamaica. The warmth of the sun, a feeling of belonging were now distant memories.

He didn't have the courage to venture outdoors, even if he wanted to, and that brought a feeling of isolation. Even the future now seemed a faraway dream, a dream without place, time, or reason.

He had time on his hands and he spent most of the day looking down at activities below; sometimes just playing with idle thoughts to pass the time away.

Then it seemed darkness fell without warning. Street lights and fog created a strange atmosphere outdoors, reflecting within him, a pensive mood. The streets gradually became deserted, silent, with a calm that seemed to pervade the whole city. It was as if everyone had suddenly gone away. This uneasy peace complemented his own feelings. He was fascinated, overcome by this strange mood. His first experience of snow had filled him with curiosity as well as melancholia. But it gave him time to think while indoors, without any clear idea of where his thoughts were leading. He looked out of the window in time to see a dog among the realm of dustbins below, its footstep barely interrupting the silence. It began to dig its way into a mound of snow, in search of food. A large pile of snow fell from a rooftop nearby and it scurried away, leaving its footprints as evidence of its visit.

He closed the curtains, climbed into bed and listened to the silence.

His neighbours were quiet. Everyone seemed to have resigned themselves to the sweetness of sleep on a wintry night. He imagined lovers cocooned in one another's arms. All he had was the warmth of the paraffin heater with its fumes, as he lay on his back, motionless, staring at the ceiling. He imagined the cracks on the ceiling to be patterns of artistry, or even a screen unto which visions of the future could be projected. It was a time for imagination on a sultry night. Thoughts about being trapped in his attic room, invaded him. He was beginning to feel sorry for himself and wanted to escape life in such a depressingly unhappy situation. He kept looking at the ceiling until the silence stole his senses and the mental anxieties disappeared with sleep.

Morning came with an abundance of rain that washed away most of the snow. There was a cold hostile wind that rattled the attic room window. He looked out of the window. People with umbrellas, head scarves and heavy overcoats, bedecked the streets. Neighbours were busy flushing toilets, running taps, preparing to face the day. For him, going outdoors would have been an exercise in determination. About mid-day the sky became reddish grey, before emptying more rain on the city. Water rushed down drains and cascaded off rooftops as melt snow crashed to the ground.

Later, when there was respite from the rain, stray dogs returned to the now exposed kingdoms of dustbins and rubbish.

The weeks that followed were almost all the same, a mixture of rain, wind, snow, and an occasional reflection that looked like the sun. Michael had by now made the mental adjustment necessary to cope with his changed condition. Then early one morning, sun filtered through the curtains of his attic room. He could see fine particles of dust floating around the room and somehow felt that today would be different. He drew the curtains to unveil that long lost, hidden secret…the sun. It was a wholly unexpected surprise.

He dressed in a hurry and went outdoors trying to shake off the negative feelings that had threatened to stifle him over the past months. He walked the streets, trying to find his way around the city and hoping for other surprises, but none came.

The rum he brought from Jamaica for Uncle Ben was long gone and Ben didn't visit too often, except when he wanted to stay with Agnes, or to make sure Michael was OK. He was busy living three separate lives. He had another lover on the other side of the city, as well as his single room in which he stayed only when he wanted solitude, or to be with men who shared the same interest, playing dominoes, drinking rum and reminiscing. He was too busy, caught up in alcoholic fantasies, to bother about paying much attention to anything else. He still made sure that Michael was safe and wasn't in need of anything although they didn't meet very often and made sure the rent for the attic room was paid and Michael had enough money.

Sweet Man had become more of a friend and mentor to Michael and the relationship became stronger as time passed. Whenever they met Michael would listen as Sweet Man explained what he called *the truth about life* and what the real world was all about. Sweet Man believed that everyone was influenced, or used by someone else, driven by self-gratification, hidden motives, desire for power, or just pure exploitation. Everyone was living in a world filled with hidden agendas and unspoken conspiracies. At the very top were those who conspired as part of a gigantic plan, and they programmed everyone to believe an eternal lie.

Somehow, some of it made sense to Michael, although he didn't understand much about political strategies, or how society worked in general. Some of the things Sweet Man said were thought provoking, some disturbing. When alone with his own thoughts, Michael often wondered how much of it made sense or why he couldn't think of something like that.

He trusted Sweet Man's wisdom and judgement; that he was honest and sincere about the things he was telling him but sometimes when he reflected on some of the things Sweet Man said, they added more tension to his over taxed mind, a mind already impacted by discontent and uncertainty.

The sun came out daily for a couple of weeks and Michael followed the same routine. Each day he went out, searching, for what, he didn't really know. He was beginning to find his way around the city and it wasn't long before he got a part time job washing dishes in a hotel. He saved his money, bought clothes and books and prepared for university.

Six months later he started studying for his law degree.

With money in his pocket, he now wanted to socialise. His motives were strong. Months of frustration without much money, or a girlfriend, being isolated; sometimes lonely, meant he was now ready for anything.

CHAPTER FIVE

The radio Uncle Ben gave Michael was playing a mixture of soul and jazz. He was in a good mood, because it was the first time he had decided to venture out on his own on a Saturday night. He had been out with Sweet Man a few times and got a lot of good advice about how to survive in the city, especially in the black community. And he'd been out several times with Linton, but never on a Saturday night. Now Linton was involved in his studies across the other side of the city and he'd decided it was time to venture out alone; to put his adventurous and survival skills to the test.

He was also buzzing for another reason. Agnes was away in Blackpool for the weekend. And although that didn't mean that he would have the freedom of the city, at least he would be free from hearing her macabre footsteps climbing the stairs towards his attic room.

Tonight he wanted to be one of the Saturday night people, to be among those looking for good music and pleasure. To him, Saturday night people seemed to know all about that. Tonight he would be one of them. He wasn't sure where to go, but he wanted to be where the music was hot, black and vibrant, and girls were available. He turned up the radio and danced his way towards the bathroom, climbed into the bath and lay there, quietly.

He closed his eyes and listened to the bebop of Charlie Parker, the alto sax riffs and motifs pulsating through his body. It brought back memories of the first time he saw a couple dancing to Parker's music. He was at a christening party with Sweet Man. The stereo was a Blue Spot Radiogram operated by a DJ wearing a pork pie hat. Well dressed and with a pseudo American accent, he put the LP on the turn table and went to the centre of the dance floor, in the middle of the room waiting for his partner to join him.

She was white. Michael was surprised to see a white woman and black man dancing to jazz from the nineteen forties and fifties. It was as if they had spent time rehearsing their routine, but was in fact entirely spontaneous. He wondered who taught white people to dance to black music. Still, it didn't matter, because she was doing all the right things.

He remembered watching closely as she arched her body and contorted it with every sound of the double bass, high hats and symbols. Every time Charlie Parker took a solo, her movements complemented each driving riff that he articulated. Her facial expressions said her soul was involved, as if she was a black ghetto child born dancing to the rhythms of black music and needed no instructions or supervision. She just let the music dictate her movements, while she registered a rhythmical ecstasy, which only music that reaches the soul can deliver. It was in her eyes, smiling face and swaying body movements.

Her partner, a better than average dancer, was tall, flamboyant. While they danced, he encouraged her with sensual sounds of approval and guided her delicately as she spun to the rhythm of the bebop. The crowd gathered round, giving them just enough space to manoeuvre, clapping and cheering as their improvised dance moves created more excitement.

As Michael lay in his bath, eyes closed, his memory charted each step, each movement. But his pleasure soon turned to disappointment when the music on the radio ended. With eyes still closed, he tried to hang on to the savour of those past memories.

The next piece of music was more placidly romantic and conjured other memories. His mind drifted to a clear pool of water - a shallow all about the same age. They were in rolled up short trousers, without shirts, and carrying sticks. The startled fish headed for deep waters and the chase ended.

There was a sudden, crashing noise, downstairs, as if something huge had fallen. The noise ejected all the previous images from his mind and he opened his eyes. It sounded as if a couple downstairs were fighting and had saved all their aggression until Agnes was away. He turned off the radio and listened. A man shouted at the top of his voice: 'What do you want me to do, rob a bank?'

He climbed out of the bath as more verbal abuse and blows were exchanged and the woman started crying. He thought, if he were an Englishman, stretched out in his bath and was interrupted by a Jamaican couple fighting, there would be hell to play. There would be a 999 call and before long the police would probably break down the door and arrest them. Here he was, looking back at pleasant moments in his life and all of a sudden, chaos downstairs.

There was another loud crash, as if a wardrobe had been toppled over, more blows, more shouted abuse.

He got dressed as fast as he could, not wanting to be around, in case things got out of hand and he had to be questioned about a murder. More importantly, he didn't want his Saturday night ruined by bad vibes. He left his attic room in a hurry and caught the train pushing whatever had taken place at Agnes's house to the back of his mind. He headed where he thought there would be a different kind of excitement, the heart of Brixton. He was determined that, nothing and no one was going to upset his upbeat mood.

The police car whizzed past, tires screeching and stopped about two hundred yards in from of him as he turned the corner and walked towards Atlantic Road. Someone across the road, upstairs, opposite where the police car stopped, turned on a light and shifted the curtains to look outside. The car doors were flung open and two policemen rushed into a passageway.

Michael kept walking, slowly. He didn't want to pass the police car until he found out what the urgency was about. There was a noise, as if someone was trying to climb over a fence. Then there were the sounds of a struggle and a policeman started cursing: 'You black fucker.'

'Bastard' said another, loudly. More verbal abuse. More blows then the scuffle was over. The policemen were now talking to each other at normal volume as they dragged a man along the ground, towards the car. Sweet Man's words echoed in Michael's ears: 'Once you are black, you are a suspect and open to abuse. You are hardly ever believed in a court of law, no matter how meritorious your conduct, especially if you are a Jamaican. Worse, once you have been arrested, they think you are a criminal for evermore.'

He started walking faster to get away from the scene, realising how easy it would be to get drawn into a confrontation and arrested. He passed the police car just as they were about to put the man inside, but carried on walking as if he hadn't noticed anything. He heard the doors slam, the engine switched on and the car accelerating at high speed. He kept walking without looking back, thinking what to do. He thought about running away, but that would probably get him arrested on suspicion, even though he wasn't breaking any law. All kinds of thoughts crossed his mind but he kept on without looking back.

The car slowed down and started curb-crawling beside him, but he looked straight ahead and kept on walking.

'Hey, you! Where you going?' It was the police officer in the back seat through his wound down window.

'Out.'

He continued walking.

'We're talking to you, Sambo.' This time the driver. The car had stopped. Michael felt he had no choice but to stop and turn around.

'Out where, Sam?'

He recognised the voice. It was the voice that had called the arrested man *black fucker*. He sounded aggressive.

An amateur boxer in Jamaica from an early age, Michael knew enough to take care of himself. But he wasn't looking for any kind of confrontation with anyone, especially with three policemen.

'Don't know where I'm going yet and my name isn't Sambo.' His response was assertive but carefully non-aggressive.

The driver and the policeman in the front passenger seat looked at each other, as if to reach agreement: *let's check him out.*

Michael kept calm as the two policemen climbed out and crossed towards him. As they came closer, he took a step backwards to give himself room to manoeuvre, if he had to do anything himself in a hurry.

The other policeman sitting in the back seat with the handcuffed man leaned out to join the conversation. 'Saturday night and you're out chasing women, right?'

'No, just going out,' was the calm response, without turning his head. The driver stared at him, sizing him up. Six feet tall and weighing about a hundred and seventy pounds. Michael radiated his long ago well-earned reputation as a fighting machine in the ring in Jamaica, an aura he tried to suppress, deeming it undesirable to test it out against three policemen. Sweet Man's words were ringing in his ears; 'You must always know when courage ends and stupidity begins.'

Without taking his eyes off the two policemen outside the car, he glanced in the back at the man they had arrested. Under the street lights, he could see him clearly. He was bleeding from the mouth and his right eye was swollen. He looked Jamaican. It was then he made up his mind that if he was going to suffer the same fate for no reason at all, it wouldn't be without a fight.

'Do you know a pimp called Leroy?' said the driver, edging closer. And where do you live?' He continued in the same breath.

Michael took another step backward but looked him straight in the eye. 'I don't know any Leroy and I live in Paddington.'

'You're out of you way, aren't you, Sam?'

'There's no law which says where I can or can't go and I don't know any pimps. Fuck you, man, just leave me alone. And my name isn't Sambo either.'

His sudden outburst took them by surprise. For a moment there was silence, as if everything including time was standing still, a kind of stalemate until the policemen looked at each other and the driver nodded his head towards the car and they got back in. He watched as they started the car.

Just before they left, the driver shouted: 'Don't pick up any white girls and let me catch you. We know all you coloured boys are pimps. This is my patch, so keep your nose clean.'

They laughed and drove off at high speed. As the car disappeared around the corner, Michael straightened his tie, buttoned his jacket and tried to adjusted his mind onto its original programme although he couldn't stop replaying the brief encounter with the police over and over as he walked.

He imagined how the situation could have ended differently. Trying to be philosophical, he thought it was his lucky night. He was out looking for excitement, but not that kind. He cleared his head and regained his composure.

Wherever there was a combination of music, alcohol, marijuana, gambling and women, there was excitement and danger. There were always people seeking pleasure from one of these sense gratifications and sometimes they end up in trouble. Sweet Man had explained all that to Michael the first night they went out together. He had introduced him to his first taste of alcohol and warned him against smoking marijuana. Marijuana was plentiful because suitcases full were brought through customs, simply because the police and custom officers didn't know enough about it. Michael knew from his days in Jamaica that people used to say smoking marijuana led to bad company. That didn't bother him though because he didn't even like smoking cigarettes.

Music was pulsating from coffee bars, seedy joints, clubs and obscure nightspots as he headed in the direction where the Saturday night people meet. Prostitutes were out looking for clients, pimps and marijuana sellers were in obscure corners watching, doing their hustling. Dice and poker players in basement flats, cellars and back rooms were trying to win small fortunes that revolved around the hustling business. You didn't have to be an expert to tell who was who. They didn't even try to hide their personas because it gave them some celebrity status.

The Christine Keeler and Mandy Rice Davies affair with Stephen Ward and John Profumo had been sensational and had put Lucky Gordon, a Jamaican, at the centre of the whole story as the alleged pimp who controlled them, as well as being a marijuana dealer. Steven Ward had lost his life because of it all but it gave plenty of lurid publicity to both marijuana and prostitution.

It was a time when everyone seemed to want to be a free spirit and didn't give a damn what the world thought. The threat of Nuclear war, the Vietnam War, or cold war with Russia, flower power, the civil rights movement, free love, the new music of the time, all seemed to generate extreme energy. It was a kind of energy that was the result of extreme fear and uncertainty. Most people were acting as if there was no tomorrow using alcohol, stimulants and free love as routes into the future.

In the heart of the city where Michael now found himself, lives could find a mixture of excitement and danger. For some, the night would probably end in a pool of their own blood because of a fight over a woman or some situation that could have been avoided. Others lived in a timeless zone where there was no difference between night and day and macho and sexual images were all important.

He stopped briefly and looked into a few places before heading for a basement flat Sweet Man had taken him to once. He stayed for only a short time and then went on to another place he had also learned about from Sweet Man that had a party most Saturday nights. It was a kind of purpose built annexe to a house, with sound proofing.

He went in, walked straight towards the bar and ordered a drink. As soon as he took the first sip, a scantily dressed white girl and her kinky looking black friend approached him. They looked like they were in their late twenties and in search of excitement. He wondered how to handle the situation. He was only twenty even if because of his size, he looked much older. He could only greet them with a wide smile, as if to demonstrate that he could handle any situation involving both of them.

'You look like a Baptist Preacher's son,' said the black girl. She moved in closer and rubbed the chilled glass with cherry brandy and ice along the contours of her face. She licked her lips at the same time, offering a clear invitation.

'Lay off him, Mary. Can't you see he's innocent?'

'Good looking as well,' said Mary, her smile full of sensuality. She burst into laughter and stared at Michael provocatively.

'No! He isn't a preacher son,' said Mary's Friend.

'What do you do, then?' She continued to display attention seeking body language.

Michael smiled and was preparing an answer but Mary interrupted. 'Want to pay for some pleasure tonight?'

'Oh shut up, Mary, he's not like that.' This girl was also looking Michael all over, with desire in her eyes.

He stood there, nonchalantly with a friendly smile; unsure how to reply. Mary's sexuality lit a spark inside his head but paying to lose his virginity wasn't an option he had had in mind before he left his attic room.

'I'm meeting someone later. I've just come in for a quick drink.' He tried to sip from his glass with some authority, as if he was in total control of the situation. He didn't want them to know he wasn't really a man of the world. He was saved by two older men walking in, becoming the focus of Mary's attention. She took her friend by the hand and said they would be back later. Before long they were in deep conversation with the two newcomers.

Michael finished his drink, glanced around admiring the other women in the place. It did so quietly, not wishing to attract attention to himself, and then he left. At the back of his mind he was thinking that, if he wasn't enjoying himself later, he might come back. He wanted excitement, but had no intention of paying for sex. Crossing swords with any of the local bad men or pimps was not a good idea either. If the likes of Mary and her friend were prostitutes, there was sure to be some pimp lurking in the shadows.

He headed for the next unknown destination.

A sound system could be heard from a fair distance. It was

pulsating and the vibrations became louder as he turned the corner. It came from a house down an alley and the door was slightly ajar. As he reached it he could feel heat and energy flowing through the open windows that were vibrating. There was laughter and excitement inside. He wasn't sure whether it was a private party but decided to take a chance and walked straight in.

There were no seedy looking characters lurking in the shadows or scantily dressed women looking for business. It was someone's birthday party with friends and family. There were friendly, smiling faces. He felt welcomed, even though a stranger. No one questioned his right to be there.

The hostess whose party it was greeted him with a smile as if he was someone she already knew. She told him her name and that it was her twenty first birthday before offering him a drink. He told her his name and congratulated her. She brought back the brandy he asked for, told him to enjoy himself and went to another guest. He felt a kind of attraction to her. She was polite and good looking. Maybe it was unconscious desire or the beginnings of infatuation. Or, was he hoping to fulfil any of the expectations he may have had of meeting woman before he left his attic room? It wasn't time for analysis. As far as he was concerned, he was out and about and was going to have a good time, whatever the outcome.

Everyone was enjoying themselves and singing to the record that was now playing:

Singer man, sing me a song
To win one soul
To win one soul
To win one soul
I hear you singing
Sweet harmony.

The DJ turned the music off momentarily and everyone continued singing:

I hear you singing
Sweet harmony...

Michael began to rock and sway to the rhythm of the singing voices, carried away by the moment and the atmosphere. He started singing along with the crowd, unable to resist the urge to dance. Nearly everyone was dancing now. Within twenty minutes, sweat was pouring down his face. It hadn't taken him long to decide that this was the place he wanted to spend the rest of the evening.

The DJ played Mento, Ska, Reggae, nineteen fifties and sixties jazz, even a few Jim Reeves records, but later on it was soul music from Wilson Pickett, Joe Tex, Otis Redding, Solomon Burke and James Brown which dominated the evening. As the night wore on, Michael eventually took a spot in a corner of the crowded room, dancing alone and wiping beads of sweat from his forehead. The hostess brought more drinks. By this time his head was buzzing with excitement.

The sensual voice came from out of the blue. 'Hello James Brown.'

Michael turned round, his eyes met hers and he didn't hesitate. They started to dance. There was a kind of instant rapport which gave him a new surge of energy. The longer they danced, the more he became captivated by her smile. The music, the moment, now fuelled by alcohol and renewed energy, soon taking complete control of his will. As they danced, he became more confident, and their dancing became more intimate. At the end of each record, he whispered in her ear: 'Can I have the next dance?' He didn't want her to walk away. But there was no need to worry because it was soon clear to him that she had no desire to dance with anyone else.

'As long as you don't plan to take out a mortgage on me all night,' came the reply. He sensed a friendly cynicism. 'Cynthia, that's my name. What about you? What do they call you?'

In a slow, warm voice, not wanting to sound dominant or overpowering, he said: 'Just Michael.'

They talked as they danced closer, feeling good with each other's closeness. He felt very optimistic now. As they danced, the earlier passions and desires he had felt revisited him. But now, it wasn't a feeling of lust. It was something more passionate, a tenderness he hadn't experienced before. As they talked and learned more about each other, they danced to everything at the same speed, dead slow. He had never been so close to a woman so warm, so sensual, and as far as he was concerned, so beautiful.

They eventually found themselves danced to Johnny Ace's 'Forever My Darling.' That stirred further tender emotions. They both knew then, that tonight, neither of them wanted to be without each other. The dimmed lights, the good music, the alcohol, the atmosphere, and Cynthia's presence, captivated his senses. Something emotionally was happening to him, something he had never known before. He didn't want to lose that feeling or pretend it didn't exist.

They left the party holding hands and Cynthia invited him back to her flat.

They spent the weekend together, treating each with enormous tenderness and sensuality. After months in his attic room, with solitude and isolation as companions, his life had suddenly changed in one evening. The negative experiences of months were erased from his mind. He wished the weekend, and how he felt, would last forever.

Although Cynthia was a few years older, he didn't care about that. She was ambitious, had a burning passion for life and wanted to be in love. She had come to England from Jamaica to study nursing, two years before he had arrived. Her life was well organised. She was certain what she wanted to do when her training was over. Like most women who came from the West Indies to study nursing in England, she was passionate about her career. Nursing was one of the better options for most women who came to England. It offered good prospects, prestige and long-term security. Factory work was the other alternative, but that had no future. Working in a factory, you could too easily be dismissed and there was very little chance of promotion.

Like so many other people who had come to England from Jamaica to work, Cynthia had a five-year plan in mind. Five years was enough time to study, have a career and save enough money before returning home to a better life. With Uncle Ben, Sweet Man and many others, that five-year plan had become a vague memory giving way to permanent residence, buying houses and producing offspring.

Michael hadn't planned to have a steady relationship with anyone, until his days as a student was over but the weekend with Cynthia somewhat changed his thinking. He felt that something special had happened to him. At first when they met, he had been driven to some extent by sexual passion and loneliness. But somehow, everything in the brief relationship felt natural.

They talked a lot about their inner feelings, expectations and dreams and a rapport grew that neither could explain. Everything was happening quickly. Whether it was love at first sight, infatuation or sexual desire, they didn't question or analyse the reasons why they so quickly felt so strongly about each other.

Monday morning came too fast. Cynthia had to be at the hospital early and he had to go to his part time job. She took him to the train station and waited until the train was on its way. He missed her from the moment the train left the station and he couldn't concentrate all day.

That evening when he returned to his attic room, Agnes was back from Blackpool.

Overtones of her voice, her familiar steps whenever she climbed the stairs, were there to greet him. To him it had ceased to matter though. His loneliness and frustrations were gone. His thoughts were now somewhere else.

CHAPTER SIX

Twelve months passed and he was still in his attic room; but only by choice. His relationship with Cynthia had become ever stronger and he could have moved into her flat if he had wanted to. But living in Paddington was ideal and he had friends and associates close by. She had made a big difference to his life and had told him she would always be there if he needed her. He felt the same way, but wanted to spend some more time on his own, and probably have another relationship before settling down. It had crossed his mind that maybe he was committing himself to a relationship too early but at the same time he found it difficult to even contemplate cheating on her when he remembered their good moments together. He felt guilty about even thinking of being disloyal to her. Meeting her had paid off. She had become the stabilising factor in his life.

He started university and with Cynthia as a positive influence, everything began to fall into place. His life now had a regular pattern, a routine. He just wanted to study, get a full time job, marry Cynthia and live ever happily after.

He still kept in touch with Sweet Man and Uncle Ben, but didn't see them too often. He was too busy pursuing his dreams and planning his long-term future. But as usual, in life, sometimes things have a way of changing unexpectedly.

It was a Thursday evening and he was in his room revising for his exams when there was an unfriendly knock at door. He opened it to find Agnes standing there, her face reminding him of the first day he met her.

'Ah want some rent.'

The first thing that came to mind was that the arrangement she had with Uncle Ben must have broken down. He looked at her for a while, wondering what to say. She waited for his answer, never for a moment losing eye contact with him. He could see she was in the mood for confrontation and wasn't going anywhere until she got an answer.

'OK,' he said, trying to sound completely sincere. 'I'll come and see you by the weekend.'

She looked at him, took a deep breath and stomped her way down the stairs. Whatever or whoever had upset her, had stirred her fighting spirit.

He closed the door and started thinking what to do. He sat on the bed, looked out of the window and watched the people and the traffic. This had become one of his habits in moments of crises or loneliness. It was a kind of therapy he had used throughout his stay in his attic room.

He made up his mind then. It was time to pack up and leave. At least he had somewhere to go and this was an emergency.

So he moved in with Cynthia.

A week after moving, he was on his way to pick up his remaining items and hand over the key to Agnes. It was a Friday evening. As he climbed the stairs he could hear Uncle Ben's voice coming from Agnes's room. He sounded angry, drunk, or both. There was also another man's voice, with a foreign accent. 'I want them out, out, damn black foreigners. What are you doing sleeping with him?'

'This is my house and they stay ef ah want em to,' said Agnes, her voice echoing through the hallway in a show her authority.

The rest of the house was quiet. Michael listened and moved closer to Agnes's door, just in case his uncle was in trouble. The shouting and arguing continued and Agnes began to cry. That surprised

Michael. He just couldn't imagine her poker face wet with tears. Not that he had anything personal against her. In more than twelve months she hadn't done a single thing for or to him, if you discounted being cold as ice and terrorising him with her mere presence but that wasn't good enough reason to dislike her as he had long ago told himself. Now he even regretted ever thinking she wasn't incapable of crying. Regardless of her personality, she was still a woman carrying all the emotional load any other woman or man might have to bear.

As he moved closer to the door to try and hear what was going on, the quarrel became more heated. From what he could hear, it seemed the man with the foreign accent was one of Agnes's other lovers Uncle Ben knew about. He thought both needed spectacles if they were fighting over Agnes. Then again, maybe underneath her abrasive, bland persona, she was an undiscovered sex bombshell. Or maybe she had a suitcase of money hidden under her bed. Obviously, both Uncle Ben and the other man thought she was worth fighting over.

'Ah shall call de pleece ef you don't go,' said Agnes.

'And I shall help you through the raas door,' yelled Uncle Ben.

There were the noises of a scuffle and Agnes screamed.

Michael started pounding the door with his fist. 'What's happening in there?' he shouted. 'Open the door.'

Neighbours were now on the landing and in the hallway. Some were peeping from slightly opened doors. There was the sound of breaking glass and a thud as someone or something fell on the floor. Agnes screaming pulled open the door. The man with the foreign accent was on the floor, blood streaming from the side of his head. Uncle Ben was standing over him with the remains of a broken bottle, cursing him and telling him to get up and fight.

Michael dragged him out of the room, pushed him towards the front door and insistently told him to wait outside.

He went upstairs, picked up the rest of his belongings and was out the front door in a few minutes but Uncle Ben was gone and he couldn't find him, so he took a taxi to Cynthia's flat.

Throughout the journey, he thought about the man lying on the floor in Agnes's room. What if he was dead? His uncle would be charged with murder and he would probably be charged as an accomplice. At least Agnes could vouch that he had nothing to do with what took place. He imagined the headlines in the newspaper: *Young Jamaican trainee solicitor abets murder.*' He tried unsuccessfully to dismiss all these negative thoughts.

The cab stopped outside Cynthia's and as he walked towards the flat he kept looking back as if to check he wasn't being followed. He went indoors, put down his belongings and peeped through the curtains. There was obviously no one outside, but anxiety was getting the better of him. He sat down on the settee and tried to control his breathing and his racing heart. What to do next?

Cynthia was at work and he wished there was someone to talk to. He poured a drink and paced the floor until he was almost exhausted from worry. He couldn't imagine where Uncle Ben could have disappeared to in such a short time. Should he have stayed at Agnes's place to make sure the man Uncle Ben hit with the bottle was OK? These were the thoughts passing through his mind before he fell asleep on the settee.

He didn't hear Cynthia come in. She stared at him sprawled out and made a small sound to wake him up.

He opened his eyes and tried to remember what had happened the night before. He was still anxious as he told her of the disturbance at Agnes's house. She tried to convince him that there was no point worrying but he felt he had a good enough reason to stay indoors all day; all weekend.

Monday morning he telephoned the university to say he wasn't feeling well and spent the whole week revising and being with Cynthia. Midday Saturday he went in search of Uncle Ben.

First he headed for Sweet Man's flat in Brixton, but Sweet Man wasn't home. He next tried some of Uncle Ben's regular places, but no one had seen him. He was almost ready to give up looking and go to the house where Uncle Ben had a rented room but as he walked towards Atlantic Road, he saw someone in the distance, resembling Sweet Man, walking into a café and he followed the man.

As he reached the cafe door he heard Uncle Ben's voice. He followed the sound and found Uncle Ben in a back room sitting at a domino table. Sweet Man was sitting next to him. Both surprised but happy to see him.

He greeted everyone, before leaning close to Uncle Ben and quietly asking about the man at Agnes's house.

'Ooo, you mean the German?'

He was talking loud enough for everyone to hear him. On cue, they were all psyched up and ready for one of his story telling sessions.

'Well, you see, me and that German sailor man go back a long, long, way. We nearly clash a few times, but nothing ever happen before the time. You know, nephew, it takes two to tangle, and more than a bottle over the head to stop one of them Hitler men. The man head hard like coconut. Believe me, nephew, it takes a lot to kill a German man. He alive and well.'

'You too old to fight with bottles and knives, Uncle Ben. Leave that to younger men,' said Sweet Man.

Uncle Ben ordered a round of drinks for everyone, including Michael, and tried to convince them that his relationship with Agnes was as good as ever. He then started talking about his Panamanian exploits and bar room brawls.

Michael took it all in as usual, but this time he had a beer in his hand and was smiling, pleased that the crisis was over and his worries unfounded. He stayed a few hours before going back home to tell Cynthia the news. In the excitement of discovering that his uncle wasn't in trouble and the German was alive and well, he forgot Cynthia would be back at work.

There was a note on the dining room table. It read: 'Love remains unchanged, even out of reach of each other's arms. It flows and will continue to flow when I see you later.'

He read the note several times, a smile on his face, thinking how lucky he was to be with someone like Cynthia. She was a lover and a friend, someone with imagination, compassion, and most important of all, they were in love. What more could he ask for? He put the piece of paper in the folder where she kept her poems and messages and opened a bottle of wine. He wanted to be with her now; to thank her, to praise her for being the kind of woman she was.

Living with Cynthia was a rewarding experience in every way. They had already learned to compromise and make the relationship work. Although, in fact, their differences were minor. They both studied and worked hard, she to become a qualified nurse and he to get his law degree. They saved their money, spent a lot of time together and were starting to make plans for a permanent future together. Despite all this lurking in the shadows of Michael's mind, were a number of insecurities and he was aware of the need to address them if things were to develop and last.

They went out regularly in their spare time and had a cross section of associates - some were black; others white and from all backgrounds. There were middle-class, privileged whites, liberals, middle-class blacks, hustlers, Greeks and Chinese gamblers, ganja sellers and smokers - all sorts. He enjoyed being in their world sometimes finding them all interesting, to say the least and sometimes a lot of fun. But he made sure he didn't get involved in any illicit or underground activities. For him, to be a lawyer and to be breaking the law wasn't his idea of common sense. He kept his mind focussed on why he had come to England.

Many of the people he met and socialised with were party people, people of the night; pleasure seekers. Most had money, or knew how to get it fast. He didn't want to live in a world where he had to save pennies every week for twenty years to live an affluent life-style but he didn't want to get involved in situations where he would put himself and Cynthia at risk. He wasn't sure how much he could earn as a solicitor in Jamaica and didn't want to be left on the bottom rung of the social mobility ladder. Still, getting caught up in the rat race, chasing his tail to keep up with the Joneses, wasn't his idea of a stress-free life either. He remained undecided about a lot of things. Despite the pressures of studying, there were parties to enjoy, fuelled with champagne, good food and great music and it didn't cost anything most of the time. He was beginning to understand the nature of the social, economic and political life in England that Sweet Man often talked about. It opened his eyes to what was happening at different levels of society and he was far from blind to the realisation that Jamaicans in England were victims of the factory system, not because of choice, but by compulsion. There was no hope of a real future in those environments.

Education was a better option. He was enjoying his lifestyle, now becoming convinced that's where he wanted to be.

Sweet Man's vision was that Jamaicans who decided to settle in England should be developing other skills to cope with changing times. His reasoning was that the system would use West Indians and abandon them when it didn't need them anymore and that Jamaican offspring would eventually be stranded on the fringes of British society if they didn't learn from their parent's experience and mistakes. These thoughts had taken root in Michael who did not want to have to hustle his way through life. He wanted to climb the social ladder with the rest but without losing touch with reality. And of course he wanted to have a good time as well.

He thought his degree would be useful, but was aware that it would take more than academic knowledge to make the world go round for him. He didn't want to become victim of a bread-winning education either for fear that it might blur his vision of what was true. He wanted to keep his identity and the truth about who he was in relation to the so called, real world. He was beginning to understand the world created for him, by those who controlled resources, the propaganda, the modus operandi which distorted the truth.

But for now, it was work, party and fun. Nothing else really significant was happening in his life. He and Cynthia had both got so involved with excitement; it seem their plans for the future were on hold.

Two years went by. They had been drifting like an uncontrollable barge, carried along in the mainstream of what was happening around them, lost in the moment but after one particular evening out, they returned home tired and in the mood to take stock.

They talked about going back to Jamaica and decided they would work two more years, save up what they could and then board a plane home. They would have enough money, would be qualified and even better still in love. They would take a holiday first, find a place to live and set up their business.

After all the good times, plans for the future was back on track.

They would get married and have children. Cynthia would practice nursing when they returned to Jamaica and he would set up a law firm of his own. He wanted them to earn and enjoy a better standard of living before he eventually became a barrister. For him, this would be a perfect ending to a pipe-dream story.

CHAPTER SEVEN

Danny Hogarth, a qualified accountant, was living and working in Birmingham. He had met Michael at university but graduated at the end of Michael's first year, moving to Birmingham from London because he thought life there would be less competitive, less demanding away from the hustle and bustle of the capital city.

The year he and Michael spent together at university was always dominated by talk about their dreams, and their desire for success. Danny wanted the fastest cars, the most beautiful women and a large bank account. The playboy image he created demanded that he make a lot of money to support his life-style. He believed that one day he would get all the things he wanted and the way to do that quickly, as far as he was concerned, was to be in control of figures and money. That was the main reason he became an accountant. Charismatic, assertive, and a womaniser, he broke a few hearts on campus, never taking relationships too seriously. Ruthless, sometimes selfish, he wouldn't let anything or anyone get in his way if he wanted something.

Danny kept in touch with Michael after he moved to Birmingham and Michael kept promising visit him for a weekend, but never managed to make it. The last time they had spoken on the telephone, Danny told him he now had a large house in the suburbs and a Mercedes. Michael couldn't figure out how that was possible in such a short time.

They had a lot in common, though Danny was born in St Lucia. Both were fatherless, from one parent families and poor backgrounds Both were ambitious. By some strange coincidence, Danny's mother had like Michael's also moved to Canada to work. His grandmother had brought him up, a common practice in the West Indies when parents travelled abroad to work while Michael had lived with his other uncle in the country after his mother went to Canada because his grandparents had died when his mother was very young.

Rather than dwelling on early misfortunes, Michael and Danny saw their experiences as assets, incentives to achieve success and they shared a lot about their backgrounds while at university.

During one of their telephone conversations, Danny hinted that he might have some work for Michael in the future. Michael didn't really give it a second thought but when Danny insisted he could earn much more than working as a lawyer, tax free, he started to reconsider. If he could get a job working with Danny in his accounting business, making good money, until it was time to leave, they would gain a much better start back in Jamaica. Curious about Danny's promise, he decided to visit him and when he telephoned Danny to say he was coming to Birmingham, Danny let out the most excited laugh.

'Brother, man, come right now. You'll get a welcome as warm as the day of the seven suns, in a city where saints and sinners have ecstatic encounters.'

He didn't know what Danny meant, but knew that he had always thought of himself as a philosopher, a metaphorical philosopher. It was a chance to break away from the lifestyle he'd established in London which, although exciting, was becoming counterproductive.

Cynthia agreed it would be a good idea, at least for a while so he packed his bags and headed for Birmingham.

He got off the train at Snow Hill station, mid-day Saturday, on a cloudless afternoon. England's second city, an industrial arena, was under tropical sunshine and clear blue sky but despite the approximation of a tropical climate, the city could not disguise its true nature. There was ample evidence of factories and smoke from the coal and coke fuelling the foundries of its main industrial concerns as a city that designed and built motor cars, machines of one kind or another, machine tools, car parts and other accessories in stark contrast to London.

Danny was at the station to meet him and they greeted each other with an enthusiastic embrace. Danny was wearing a silk shirt and smart lightweight mohair suit, the latest style. He looked like a successful businessman. Michael was much more casually dressed.

They were both excited as they walked towards the car, eager to tell each other what they'd been doing in recent times. It was more than four years since they had seen each other and they were eager to celebrate their reunion. As they approached a row of cars parked up ahead, Michael couldn't help noticing the Mercedes. It was metallic blue and spotless. To his surprise Danny stopped by the driver's door and said, 'This is it, man.'

Michael stepped back to admire the car, a look of surprise and admiration on his face. They walked around it scrutinising every detail.

'Like it?' asked Danny. The glow of pleasure on his face as he smiled, was almost competing with the brilliance of the sun and the sheen of the paintwork.

'No, man, I love it?' said Michael with justified over exuberance.

'You could be driving one just like this, man, just like this. All you need is patience and work that earns you real money.'

'If you've got the work I've got the patience, man.'

They laughed loudly as they got into the car.

The luxury of the Mercedes suggested that the owner had taste and style. The sunroof was the latest model and the interior was impressive. The seats were pure leather. Michael was amazed and pleased that Danny had made such progress as to be able to afford an expensive Mercedes. At University he had worn jeans and moccasins and was usually unshaven. Now he was wearing an expensive, multi-coloured tie and gleamingly polished alligator skin shoes. His Rolex watch was the same colour as the Mercedes.

Danny turned up the volume on the radio, accelerating along the dual carriageway on the way home.

Michael felt a sudden rush of adrenalin hit him. 'What happened, Danny? Tell me, man!'

'Brother, man, this is me!' A broad grin on his face.

'Yea, but what really happened?'

'I woke up one morning and found myself in a big house with a beautiful wife and a Mercedes parked outside, man. I was just as surprised as you are now.'

'I suppose you woke up with the suit on as well?'

'No, man, serious! I just did some reasoning and decided we can't all work for British Rail, drive buses, or work in hospitals and factories. You can't pretend to be successful if you're at the bottom of the heap. That's part of my story.'

Michael nodded in acknowledgement. 'Yea! You into drugs, Danny?'

'No, man! Don't do drugs. I'm an accountant. Remember? I got some quick money, invested it in a business, and presto.'

'Just like that?

'Yea...Just like that, man.'

'Maybe I should invest some money if business is that good. What about the risk?'

'Brother, man, when you go to sleep at night, there's a risk of falling out of bed or not waking up. The ceiling could cave in on you. So what the hell? Everything in life has risks. Anyway, no business talk tonight, man, just pleasure.'

'Yea,' agreed Michael and then they were both laughing again.

Danny might not be going out of his way to impress Michael but was displaying an enticing air of success and Michael could not be other than impressed. As far as Michael was concerned, Danny hadn't changed but seemed to have found success even though he was just as flamboyant and full of confidence as on the first day they had met.

They listened to Otis Redding on the radio singing: 'I Can't Get No Satisfaction' telling each other some of the things they had done since leaving university. What Michael had achieved didn't seem to amount to much in comparison to Danny but Danny reassured him that he would show him how to make, fast.

The driveway that led to Danny's front door was flanked by well-kept gardens. There was a tennis court and swimming pool. It definitely wasn't the kind of house Michael expected a black man living in Birmingham to own. It looked out of reach, off limits, a place you would expect to be owned by an aristocrat or a film star. Even though he knew Danny wasn't the type of man that believed in limitations, what he had achieved in such a short time was beyond Michael's wildest expectations but then he remembered Danny once telling him, 'If you limit yourself, you lose sight of your objectives. If you think hard enough about what you want, providence will find a way to make things materialise.'

Thoughts had really materialised for Danny and Michael was happy for him and proud of his success. He was proud to find that he wasn't feeling a hint of jealousy or envy either. It was just that he felt disappointed with his own lack of achievement. Everything he had seen since he got off the train and met Danny again suggested that he had been wasting time all these years.

Michael stepped out of the car in surroundings that were far removed from anywhere he had been in London. He took a panoramic view, admiring everything he could see. There was a complete absence of noise and pollution from traffic or factories. The nearest industrial estate was miles away from this exclusive area. They both stood in silence with broad smiles and looked around them, Danny's smile bordering on smugness.

'Like it?'

Michael didn't hesitate. He gave instant approval, nodding his head and saying, 'Yea, yea.'

It was a good feeling, knowing that he had a friend living in an exclusive part of Solihull but it reinforced a sudden urge to do something to improve his own life.

Barbara, Danny's wife, emerged from the front door to greet them. Walking towards the car she was black, beautiful and not what Michael had expected. He had never met her before and Danny had never said anything about her during their telephone conversations. Seeing the house and the surroundings he had half-expected a middle-aged, white woman to come to the front door; someone much older than Danny. Perhaps, a woman prepared to part with her fortune for the favours of a good looking, virile black male who might fulfil some of her fantasies. Danny had always had an unconcealed liking for English women and had had a lot of white female admirers. Michael had assumed that would continue.

Instead, Barbara was black, in every sense of the word, without a trace of European blood in her complexion. Dressed in traditional African clothes, her gracefulness was that of a woman well cultured. Her smile had no trace of arrogance or insincerity and she walked with elegance and a poise that were neither frivolous nor mechanical.

As she shook Michael's hand, Danny introduced her as Princess Ayesha. She corrected that to *Barbara*, although Michael later discovered she was from a long line of African royalty.

They went indoors and Danny steered Michael straight to the bar while Barbara prepared dinner.

After their first drink, Danny took Michael on a tour of the house. There were five large bedrooms, two lounges, a living room and a library. All were beautifully decorated with expensive furniture and paintings. As Michael walked around the house with Danny, admiring the exquisite surroundings, he could see the pleasure of ownership in Danny's eyes. Michael just couldn't help thinking, *How could this all come about so quickly?* To him, it didn't seem possible that an accountant could accumulate such wealth and live in his present surroundings in such a short time. Perhaps Barbara was the source of his wealth. He told himself that it was none of his business, though he was still curious.

When he asked the question, Danny told him that Barbara was a high profile marketing executive, working for a multi-national company. She had lots of privileges and knew people in high places. Whatever the circumstances, they were clearly both living a successful life.

The house was such a complete contrast to the flat Michael and Cynthia were living in. It was small and with few facilities, a far remove from the tasteful and lavish surroundings he now found himself occupying. His guest bedroom overlooked open fields and he could imagine himself being on holiday in a foreign country.

Barbara didn't object when Danny told her he was taking Michael out for the evening. She seemed happy he had linked up with an old friend and kept insisting there was plenty of room in the house and he could stay as long as he liked. Dinner was a pleasant affair, with African cuisine. Michael felt a warm sense of welcome both from the traditional food and Barbara's explanations of African traditions and customs. It was not that Michael was unaccustomed to African practices. In Brixton he had African friends, mainly Nigerians, many of them in the same predicament as Jamaicans there. Trying to survive and entertaining themselves, were two of their first priorities. What astonished him was the grace of Barbara's hospitality.

After dinner, Barbara went off to a business meeting and after more drinks, they got dressed up and Danny took Michael into the city.

Michael was already looking forward to a surprise party Danny had promised him. He watched houses and buildings whizz by from the passenger seat of the Mercedes wondering just what Danny had meant earlier when he mentioned *the delights of the city*. He had used a similar phrase to Michael the week before on the telephone.

The evening sun was bright and the prelude to the evening was a tour in the Mercedes. They drove through villages, small towns and built up areas before heading towards the city centre. Danny slowed down so Michael could admire the blend of people in their latest and different fashions. People were walking in the evening sunshine, as if the sun was a phenomenon they were out to worship, a rare commodity; a kind of deity who only visited every so often. Michael guessed that most were out to enjoy an intoxicated Saturday night, for the atmosphere, stimulants and pleasure.

They reached the heart of the city amidst slow moving traffic. The music from the Mercedes car radio and the clicking of shoe heels on the pavements, created a cacophony of rhythmic sounds. It gave a feeling of activity and expectation. Michael anticipated a great night ahead.

Danny was rocking to the music and humming the melody of the song on the radio. Traffic was now almost at a standstill. They were in the middle of the city full of people caught up in a night for wishes and desires. Some would become invisible by disappearing into small corners and private places, unnoticed, except by those close enough to taste the warmth of their breath and feel their heartbeats. Others would probably wander aimlessly and return home to empty houses and apartments, intoxicated by one thing or another or overwhelmed by loneliness.

They decided to head for Handsworth, the heart of the West Indian community, the *Front line* and chose to go first to the Continental Club on the Soho Road. It was one of Danny's regular hideaways from the exclusive aspects of where he now lived. For some people it was a halfway house, on their way to somewhere, or when returning from somewhere else. Most things you wanted for the evening were there, alcohol, music, gambling, marijuana, women and entertainment. For some, Saturday night started and ended there.

The bar was crowded with well dressed women, some giggling with excitement, while others rocked and swayed to the music. Some had cigarettes or spliffs in their hands or hanging from their lips. Danny and Michael struggled through the crowd as they headed for the bar to buy drinks, and stand admiring the women, before moving on into another more spacious room. From there they could see a crowd of men, different ages and nationalities, standing around a dice table. The gamblers included loose-talking, free argument 'Rude Boys,' businessmen and hustlers. There were Asians, Greeks, whites, Africans, but mainly Jamaicans. All seemed to be members of the underground economy and night ravers, their main interests being money, sex, music, pleasure, alcohol, not necessarily in that order. There were many similarities to Brixton.

Some Rude Boys were in a corner, looking cool, observing and listening to what was going on. 'De revalushan muss come,' said one, wearing a sheep skin jacket and Pork Pie Hat.

'Wah kinda revalushan?' someone in the background shouted.

'Who gwine to lead it, you?' said another voice, full of sarcasm and laughter.

A man, who it became apparent was simply known as Bigger because his size and the volume of his voice overshadowed everyone, said, 'All I man believe in is money. My money is my friend, my politics, my revalushan. I don't wah live and fight like nuh white man. I man fight if I have a good reason. But all I want right now is some good runnings fe me an my pickney dem. You see it?'

Mikey T, a slick dresser with a 'Skiffle' haircut, took the dice cup from the table and said: 'All I man want right now is some hot money. Right now! Dice ah beg bread.' He shook the cup and threw the dice on the table. The dice played seven. He took a handful of notes from his pocket, tossed them on the table and started soliciting, chanting to invite customers. He took up the money from the table, threw it down again and shouted: 'Bet!'

Just then two Greeks walked in the room. One had a bottle of whisky in his hand and the other was smoking a Cuban cigar. The man smoking the cigar made sure everyone noticed his expensive gold watch and bracelet. As if to attract further attention, he took a silk handkerchief from his pocket and wiped his sweaty hands. His overgrown stomach was ruining his nicely pressed suit.

Mikey T, took more notes from his pocket and threw then on the dice table. He seemed excited at the prospect that an Aristotle Onassis equivalent had just walked in with all the funds from his shipping company.

Another man approached the table. He was greeted by somebody, as *Nigerian Joe*. Wearing traditional African clothes, he was accompanied by a stiletto-heeled, permed-hair, mini skirted, white girl. She was clutching his arm and attracted even more attention than the Greeks.

Michael and Danny sipped their drinks without talking and kept their eyes and ears tuned to the drama around them. Nigerian Joe took a bundle of money from his pocket and threw it down next to Mikey T's money on the table and said only, 'Bet.'

The croupier took control of the game and the Greek with the bottle of whisky came closer. Mikey T shook the dice cup long and hard before bouncing the dice off the sides of the table. They spun and played two sixes. Before long large sums of money were exchanging hands. One of the Greeks went outdoors to his car and brought back a brief case. He opened it on the dice table and it was full of money. Everyone was now eager to get involved and before long the game was in full flow, financed by the underground economy. The music was hot and everyone seemed to be having a good time.

Michael and Danny went back to the bar and started talking to two girls. One was an incessant giggler. All four were in polite conversation when two very huge men walked over to Danny who introduced them to Michael as Billy and Frank. Billy was white with long, blonde hair. Frank was mixed race. They were both about six feet four. They said 'Hello,' and then took Danny outdoors to have a conversation. They came back after a few minutes and Danny apologised but soon afterwards asked to be excused and went outdoors again, this time leaving Michael with

Billy and Frank, two total strangers. He wasn't quite sure how to begin a conversation but it eventually got off the ground with Michael telling them how much he was enjoying his weekend in Birmingham. They didn't ask a lot of questions; neither did Michael but at least Billy seemed interested in talking about Birmingham and how exciting a city it was. Michael told them a bit about life in London although he felt sure they knew much more about what was happening in London than he did. Danny came back after perhaps ten minutes to rescue him from what had become a boringly artificial conversation. He felt relieved when Danny said it was time to go. They left shortly after.

Michael's mind was pre-occupied by a lot of thoughts as they drove towards the hotel which was their pre-planned last stop before going to the party. Cynthia was on his mind even as they talked and listened to the radio. He hadn't even telephoned her to say he had arrived safely in Birmingham. He was also thinking about the unexpected appearance of Billy and Frank, their discreet conversation and Danny's disappearance outdoors. He wasn't too preoccupied: he was sure Danny would probably explain everything at a convenient time and nothing was going to affect their high spirits as they headed towards the hotel.

The hotel bar was crowded. The music was good and so was the atmosphere. They found cosy seats next to two attractive girls Danny knew. Pamela was from Birmingham and Judy had a Liverpool accent. They were out for a good time and weren't making any efforts to disguise their intentions. Danny ordered two bottles of champagne and the girls started behaving as if they had found their dates for the evening. He had to make it clear that he had plans later, which didn't include them. The girls just drank the champagne as fast as they could, obviously hoping that Danny would change his mind about later.

An hour passed, drinking with humour, titillation and sweet talk about nothing much in particular. Michael was enjoying himself, but wasn't allowing himself to be over-impressed with the girls' advances. He had no desire for anything which would constitute disloyalty to Cynthia. The champagne, music, conversation and atmosphere was stimulating enough but he knew too much champagne had the power to lead to other things.

To Michael's surprise Billy and Frank arrived. He watched their progress through the crowded lounge, saw them buy and then they headed in his and Danny's direction. To Michael, their smart appearance didn't disguise who they really were. Even immaculately dressed, they looked like rough and ready villains, similar to some of the same he'd met in London. He felt a little uneasy at seeing them again, but tried not to show his feelings. When they sat down at the table, he noticed a scar on Billy's right cheek, which he hadn't spotted before. Frank's hands also had scars, like a boxer's. They both had obviously been involved in a few wars whether inside or outside the ring.

Danny ordered more Champagne and the girls were giggling even more with Billy and Frank taking an interest in them. Michael was hoping they would take the girls with them when they left but neither Pamela or Judy were interested. Their new arrivals had somehow put a slight edge on the atmosphere. Michael was quietly pleased when they decided to leave, *on a mission*, as Frank explained. They seemed friendly enough as they shook hands with everyone at the table, but their manner still somehow looked menacing as they made their way towards the exit.

Pamela and Judy did end up leaving the hotel with Michael and Danny. By this time their heads were fully loaded with champagne and Judy opened her handbag on the way to the car and took out two ganja spliffs. They were as long as the Cuban cigar the Greek had been smoking in the Continental Club. She lit one for herself and handed the other to Pamela. They got into the back of the Mercedes and the giggling recommenced.

The car radio was on as they drove towards the city. The girls were chatting quietly - finalising their entrapment plans for the evening perhaps. The conversation between them soon became noisy laughter and Danny decided they were in no shape to be abandoned alone in the city and agreed to take them to the party.

Michael was silent, his eyes focused on the road ahead as they drove along.

Danny broke his silence. 'Brother, man, you're quiet.'

The remark interrupted his concentration. 'Just thinking, man.'

'Tonight's not the night for thoughts, just action, man. Pure, raw action.'

Michael burst into laughter, repressing and failing the urge to ask about Billy and Frank. As Danny lit a cigarette and changed gear to take a corner, Michael asked, 'Those guys - Frank and Billy - are they your close friends?'

'No! Just some guys who work for me.' Danny was glancing in his mirror as he answered, as if to divert Michael's interest in another direction entirely.

'What kinda work?'

'Bit ah this, bit ah that.'

'Like what?'

'Depends. In this city, there's every kind of work.'

'Outside the law?'

'Take your pick. I'll tell you what, though, sometimes people who operate outside the law make the most money.'

The girls in the back were giggling again and Danny killed the conversation by calling out to them, flirting to change the mood. He accelerated, as if fuelled by a rush of adrenaline and turned up the stereo.

Michael kept his eyes on the road, his mind in overdrive, but feeling happy enough. He was still high on champagne. As they cruised along, he had the feeling Danny was reflecting and wondered what was going through his mind. Then he remembered what Danny had said earlier: *tonight wasn't a night for analysis. It was a night for raw action.*

The Mercedes stopped in front of a set of large iron gates. Someone who obviously knew Danny, greeted him, opened the gates and told him where to park. He put the Mercedes between two other expensive cars, a Rolls Royce and another top of the range Mercedes.

The house was a large, English country mansion, much bigger than Danny's. The surrounding areas were brightly lit, with neatly designed lights that highlighted well-kept gardens.

They arrived in an expensively decorated hallway with several oil paintings on the walls. Inside the house seemed even larger than it had looked from the outside. There were several rooms on either side of the hallway, all with open doors. There was music, alcohol, food, and any number of people in each room. The evening and the house had been plainly organised to impress as soon as anyone walked through the door.

The main party was in a very large room with lots of champagne, expensive wines, spirits and food to satisfy nearly every taste. Women of different complexions and from varying backgrounds were there in abundance. Some were wearing traditional dress;

others mini, midi and maxi skirts.

The men too were from all backgrounds and ages, some in smart Italian-made suits, others in turbans or African traditional dress and there were a number of Jamaicans, easily identified by their own style, body language and accents. Pamela and Judy seemed overawed by the whole setting but made a valiant attempt to display composure, given how drunk they already were.

Michael wasn't too fazed, although it was more outlandish than he might have imagined. He had developed a taste for lavish life-style through friends in London, but this was at a different level again. Danny introduced him to some personal friends and told him to feel free to move around and meet people. Pamela and Judy had already wandered off to the champagne bar. The sight of beautiful women and the sound of good music were both intoxicating. There was a live band playing soul music in another room close by.

Danny introduced Michael to more interesting people who included civil servants, a professional boxer, businessmen, solicitors, and even some street-wise hustlers. Most were eager to talk about themselves, to feel important. Many seemed to know each other, for one reason or another.

Michael had the feeling there was a kind of special relationship between most of the people, that they were a clutch of friends and associates, regardless of their various backgrounds. The champagne was also helping him to get rid of any inhibitions he might have had.

He ended up in a corner, with a bottle in his hand of a good vintage, *Bollinger Vielles Vignes Francaises*. He watched Pamela as she danced with an Asian man making a bad job of twisting to a Chubby Checker song. Each time the record stopped playing, Pamela would down another drink as fast as she could.

Danny was at a bar opposite, surrounded by admirers. His friends were slapping him on the back in admiration and sharing laughter. For the moment, Michael felt secure in the shadows. He was out to have fun, but he wanted to see things from a distance, as an outsider.

Judy joined Pamela on the dance floor and her movement away from him enabled Billy to spot Michael, although he was barely visible in his dimly lit corner. Billy too had a bottle of champagne in his hand and he was filling his glass as he reached Michael. 'Having a good time?'

'Great, man,' said Michael, sipping his champagne and swaying his body to the music.

Billy tried a few movements but might as well have been taught to dance by a couple of Russian dancing bears, as far as Michael was concerned. He invited Michael to a table in another room that was less crowded. He said he wanted to talk. Michael couldn't guess why. They had after all only met for the first time that evening at the *Front Line*, a few hours earlier. Michael thought Billy a boring conversationalist and didn't think he would be any better after a few drinks. He certainly didn't want to hang around with him too long. He decided to jump-start the conversation as soon as they took a seat.

'Whose party is it?'

'The boss.' Billy pointed to a huge man in a pin-striped suit in the opposite room. 'That's him over there, Mr Anastasia.'

Michael nodded to acknowledge he had seen him.

Billy told him that he would do all right if he came to Birmingham and that Mr Anastasia had a big business organisation, with plenty of work and money for the right man. He became excited, even animated, as he tried to convince Michael he would be better off in Birmingham.

Michael was curious and wondered why Billy was giving him all this information when surely he should be hearing this from Danny. Maybe Danny had sent Billy to talk to him.

Billy gave some background to Mr Anastasia's lifestyle and his organizations. It just wasn't the kind of information you give to a total stranger. Billy told him how rich Mr Anastasia was, that he had many people working for him and had lots of businesses all over the place. Michael was beginning to wonder if Billy was stupid, or was trying to impress him for some unknown reason. He was saying much more than Mr Anastasia or Danny would probably want him to. He took it all in and came to the conclusion that Mr Anastasia couldn't possibly be totally legitimate. And if that was the case, he guessed, neither was Danny.

Then he thought, maybe Billy was just high on champagne like everyone else. That might have loosened his tongue. Still, he knew that Danny had a brilliant mind and was entirely capable of planning and engineering this whole scenario between Billy and himself. He kept sipping his champagne taking in the information Billy was providing and trying to see how things added up. He came to the conclusion that Mr Anastasia was a kind of Godfather.

Eventually Billy left to talk to other friends and Michael decided it was time to start enjoying himself. That wasn't difficult. The champagne was doing its job and he was ready to be lured into unknown, less safe, territory. He was on his way to re-join Danny when Judy grabbed him, working overtime on winning his affections. Danny came to the rescue in time, took him by the arm, apologised for abandoning him, and started introducing him to more friends. Soon he was dancing with a couple of elegant, well-dressed and highly perfumed women. He made promises to them that he would keep in touch at some later date but had no intentions of keeping any of those promises.

Danny again came to his rescue, threw his arms around his shoulder and steered him towards another room along the hallway. They were both in vibrant mood.

'What do you think of the party, brother, man?'

'Cool as ice, man! Yea I'm enjoying myself,'

'You see any girls you like?'

'All of them, man, but nothing doing. I've got a nice lady in London and I don't want to spoil things.'

'It's not Janet who used to have a crush on you at university, is it?'

'No, nothing went down between us, man. She was just a good friend.'

'A teaser who wouldn't deliver?'

'Nothing like that, man. She was just a good friend.'

'I see Billy was talking to you.'

'Yea, he was just saying you might have a lot of work for me.'

'I didn't give Billy any message to give you, man. Billy is just an impulsive guy with a few grey matters missing. Thinks he's Einstein. But he's tough. Used to work with racehorses as an assistant trainer. Sometimes he behaves as if he's got horse shit for brains. But he's OK and reliable. Just tell him what to do and he'll do it. Listen, man, you see all the things I've got, you can have the same in a few years. Solicitor's fee can't buy the things you see around you.'

Just then a Nigerian girl, almost as beautiful as Barbara, joined them and Danny introduced her as a friend of Barbara's. The party was in full swing and nearly everyone was now dancing. 'Why don't you two dance?'

'It depends on whether Naptali wants to dance with me.'

Her response was immediate and enthusiastic. 'I would love to. Your friend looks as if he can handle himself on the dance floor.'

Danny went to the DJ and asked him to put on some *High Life*, African music. Soon Michael and Naptali became the main focus on the dance floor. Naptali knew all the intricate movements of African traditional and High Life music and Michael soon found himself in uncharted dance territory. Only the little he had learned from dancers in Brixton, rescued him from complete embarrassment but a crowd gathered around Michael and Naptali, cheering them as they danced to the insistent rhythms.

When the music ended, Danny and Mr Anastasia, who had a large cigar hanging from his lips, walked towards them. Mr Anastasia's huge hand with its sausage-like fingers was extended to shake Michael's hand as he congratulated them both on their dancing skills. and invited both of them to have a drink with him.

They could hardly reject the invitation and followed Mr Anastasia to another bar in a private room. There were two bodyguards shadowing him from a close distance. One looked like a Mongolian Karate expert, a cousin of the great *Todo* the wrestler, Oddjob in the James Bond movie. Michael thought he was the type to avoid at all cost or someone to ensure was on your side if trouble broke out.

'This is the friend I was telling you about, Mr Anastasia, he's from London,' said Danny.

'Oh, a Londoner! We could do with some London people in our business. They're smart people.'

'I'm Jamaican. I was a student, but my studies are finished and

I'm planning to go back to Jamaica soon.'

'Jamaican eh? I know a lot of smart Jamaicans. I'm Greek. I live in Birmingham and I'm going nowhere.' He spoke with an air of total confidence. 'What did you study?'

'Law,' said Michael, not trying to sound cocky or self-assured.

'Law eh? You know' I could do with a good lawyer around here.'

'I'm not a practising lawyer, I've only got a degree.'

'Well, my boy, we've all got to start somewhere. Danny said you're bright and might be looking for work. I could do with a few more intelligent men like Danny around me. What kind of work you looking for?'

'Any kind, not too back breaking but work that pays real money.'

'Well my boy, I've got all kinds of jobs, especially for a smart young mind like yours. I like a man with brains as well as brawn. And what's all this nonsense about going back to Jamaica? Jamaica is a British colony and you have a British Passport, don't you?'

'I've got a Jamaican Passport which says I'm a British subject and a Citizen of the United Kingdom and Colonies.'

'Well why don't you relax and stay for a while? You can come and go as you like, can't you?'

'Yes, but that might change now that Jamaica got independence.'

'Let's have a drink and stop talking politics. Politics is for the politicians. I'm a businessman.'

At the merest gesture from his boss a waiter brought a tray over with four glasses and another bottle of expensive champagne. The next twenty minutes were spent talking about different things until Naptali took it into her head to suggest that Mr. Anastasia could start a business in Nigeria and Danny agreed it was a good idea.

Just then, an elegantly dressed woman came over and whispered something in Mr Anastasia's ear. He asked to be excused, but before he left with his glamorous messenger now clinging to his arm, he said, 'I hope you like Birmingham. No point rushing back to London or Jamaica when you can enjoy some of the good things in this city. My business could use a man like you. And you won't be short of money or beautiful women. Have a good evening.'

Michael watched them leave, the woman still clinging to Mr Anastasia's arm. Naptali was still clinging to him and not hiding the fact that she was enjoying his company but that was interrupted by one of her friends who wanted a private conversation with her.

Danny seemed pleased that Mr Anastasia had taken an apparent liking Michael and was quick to seize the opportunity to reignite Michael's interest. 'As long as you ride with me you're cool, man. There's nothing to worry about. Let's drink.'

He was in no mood to resist that invitation. With all the champagne he already had, he felt halfway to paradise. He felt he could fly to the moon without a rocket. It had been an enjoyable evening after a long and tiring day but he had not neglected at any point to note down useful telephone numbers for people he wanted to keep in touch with and he'd filled a complete page in his little pocket memo book.

Pamela and Judy were in much worse shape than Michael or Danny. They appeared completely exhausted, looking more than a little the worse for wear so Danny offered to drop them off en route. It was nearly sunrise when they said farewell to Naptali with Danny promising to invite her for dinner soon.

They headed home.

CHAPTER EIGHT

Amazing grace,
How sweet the sound,
That saved a wretch like me,
I once was lost but now I'm found,
Was blind but now I see.

Michael sat up in bed, his head throbbing from the previous night's abuse of alcohol. He tried to figure out where the singing was coming from. He knew it wasn't from a mission house in Trench Town, because the voice didn't have a Jamaican accent and the surroundings were far removed from that sort of location. He looked around the room and tried to clear his head.

Finally he recognised Barbara's voice. She was singing as loud as she could, with all the power and effort of someone rehearsing for an opening night on Broadway. It was as if she was a messenger from God, sent to punish him and Danny for staying out late and drinking too much. She was preparing to go to church and tuning up her voice.

Michael's head ached, the room smelled of alcohol and there was a terrible taste in his mouth. He could also hear Danny snoring.

'Danny,' shouted Barbara, causing Michael yet more anxiety as her voice echoed through his throbbing head.

Danny's snoring continued relentlessly, at the same pitch and rhythm.

'Danny!' This time Barbara's voice went up a register and echoed through the whole house.

'What's the problem?' croaked Danny.

'You're snoring,'

Danny was silent for a while; then the snoring started again. When Barbara called the third Time he stumbled out of bed and went to the bathroom. He was mumbling to himself as he flushed the toilet.

'What do you want, Barbara?'

'I just told you. You're snoring.'

'Is that all?'

'Isn't that enough? You're making enough noise to wake the whole neighbourhood. Don't forget we've got a guest.'

'He's not a guest, he's a friend and he's not complaining.'

'That's because he's too polite to complain. Breakfast is nearly ready. I'll bring it up in twenty minutes.'

Michael was hoping that Barbara wouldn't bring any breakfast for him. He had no desire to eat. Nor did he think he had the strength. Twenty minutes later when he heard footsteps coming up the stairs, he feared the worst. The smell of coffee, green bananas, ackee and salt fish wafted through the doorway ahead of Barbara with a heaped tray of food. He struggled to open his eyes.

'I know that you men like to over indulge in alcohol, even though you know you will suffer later. Now eat up you'll feel better soon. I'll be back for the tray before I go to church.'

She started singing again as she walked away, but this time her voice was much softer, a soothing rendition of the same hymn.

Michael was having a shower when he heard the front door slam. When he got back to his bedroom the tray was gone, the bed neatly made and several Sunday papers were on the bedside table. One carried a story about Ronnie Biggs, the great train robber who was still being hunted by police but was hiding away safely in Brazil.

Another paper ran a follow up story on the Profumo scandal. While he was browsing through the papers, his Sunday morning was again interrupted, this time by the sound of a vehicle outside the front door.

The doorbell rang. He looked out of the window to see a shaven head, on a huge frame. The man was white and weighed about three hundred pounds. Well over six feet tall, his face looked like he had collided at some point in the past with a freight train.

The repeated sound of the doorbell startled Danny awake and he staggered downstairs for a short conversation with *Shaven Head*, in the hallway. After that the huge man went back to his Range Rover and sped away.

'Who was that?'

'Oh, just Pete.'

'You sure know some weird looking characters.'

'Pete's OK. He's rough, but he's a nice guy. Got some brains as well.'

'Bet he could scramble a few brains!'

'Yea he's seen off a few guys in his time. Used to be a heavy-weight champion wrestler.'

'I hope I don't ever get to grips with the likes of him, Frank or Billy in a dark alley.'

'You don't have to worry about them. I've got guys who can take care of them all if they step out of line.'

'Must be important to be calling this early on a Sunday morning.'

'They've got some backlog, urgent work and need somebody fast. Not the kind of work you could handle.'

'I can handle anything, man, as long as the money is right.'

'You interested?'

'Sure. As long as the money is OK and I don't have to break anybody's leg for it.'

'You won't have to worry about that.'

'You mean you've already got your own leg breakers?' He was trying to conjure an air of good humour, although his head was still throbbing persistently.

'All you would have to do is work, and keep cool, man. You could make some real money, fast.'

He tried to think why everyone was so eager to give him a job. He had only just arrived in Birmingham. Everything was happening too soon; too fast. 'What kind of work, Danny?'

'Painting, brother, man.'

'But I've never even painted a gate post.'

'The job is spraying cars and it won't take a smart guy like you long to learn.'

'But I've never sprayed a car in my life.'

'What they want is someone reliable, someone who can be trusted and I trust you. You'd start getting good money from day one, even while you're learning.'

'As long as you remember that I'm a lawyer, man.'

'You want to earn some real money, don't you?

'Well, yea.'

Danny went into the shower and Michael was left in limbo. He needed to earn and this was a big new chance but he just couldn't imagine how he would earn a lot spraying cars. Before he left London for Birmingham, his plan was to hold on to his part time jobs for at least another year. Now he was prepared to give those up if Danny was offering something worthwhile financially. He would then return to Jamaica and practice law with a small company before opening his own business. He knew that nothing was guaranteed back in Jamaica and taking a decent amount of money home would guarantee survival and a better standard of living, at least for some time. For that he was prepared to take a chance, as long as he wasn't mixed up in anything that would get him into real trouble. He thought, *Why not?* He didn't really want to live the kind of lavish life-style Mr. Anastasia or Danny enjoyed but working for a better standard of living and a successful business when he returned to Jamaica – that was worth an element of risk.

Danny turned off the shower and was on his way to his bedroom when Michael confronted him on the landing. 'How much money, Danny? How much does the job pay?'

'About £50 a week while you're learning. After that you get paid for each car you do. Real money. If you can't handle it, no problem. I'll find you another job. But I need someone real quick, someone I can trust. It's urgent.'

He took a while before he answered. The kind of money Danny was offering was a small fortune to him. The amount of money took him by surprise and he tried to figure out how many cars a week he would be able to spray. 'Yea, I can handle it, man.'

'When you know the job, you'll get a bonus as well and more money. And there are other jobs you might like doing.'

'Not bad! Better than working as a lawyer,' Michael said, trying to disguise his enthusiasm and his natural sense of curiosity. He was thinking what kind of car could cost that kind of money to spray.

He joined in Danny's laughter as his friend ransacked the medicine cupboard to find something to cure his hangover.

'Don't mention any of this to your girlfriend or Barbara. No special reason. I just want to keep this between you and me. You know how it is with some women. You should tell them what you're doing but not everything. If you feel up to it, do the job, collect your money and keep cool, man. It's like the good old days. Only, this time, we're dealing with real money rather than intellectual ideas. Later on I'll show you how to invest in some business. Don't forget I'm an accountant.'

'How can I forget?' He glanced at the painting on the wall as he responded. It was a copy of the Laughing Cavalier. Michael knew that sometimes when you ask questions, you get answers you don't want to hear. He didn't want to ask too many questions - just enough to make sure he didn't end up in a shallow grave somewhere. As far as he was concerned, all he wanted to do was to work and earn some tax-free money, to carry out his long-term plans.

Back in his bedroom, he tried to read the Sunday papers, but his mind kept wandering. Some of Danny's associates looked dangerous and he felt sure there were more than enough real villains hidden behind the scene but he also knew from past experience, that the promise of money had the power to drive away fear, or to put it on the back burner temporarily. He was going to try his luck, at least for a short while. If things weren't working out, he would pack his bags and take a train back to London.

There was no more talk about work the rest of the day. Instead they had a few beers to get rid of their hangover and talked about the past and all the other things men talk about in the absence of women. It was a sunny afternoon and they sat in the garden and whiled the time away, reminiscing. All Michael's fears and apprehensions disappeared for the moment, washed away by beer and malt whisky.

Barbara returned home from Church late afternoon and prepared dinner. For Michael, the taste of Barbara's cooking again was in itself worth the trip to Birmingham.

During dinner, Danny was eager to talk about how well off and well known Barbara's family was in Nigeria while she didn't seem to want to spend time talking about herself. Instead, she wanted to know more about Michael's background and was keen to meet Cynthia.

Michael learned from Danny's boasting on her behalf that Barbara had come to England to study economics and then worked as a consultant and trouble shooter for well-known companies. Now that she and Danny were together, it seemed that the combination of their economic and accountant qualifications were paying dividends.

Stories of African and Caribbean history and culture were shared after dinner and they all agreed they had plenty in common. Barbara's wish was to go back to Nigeria to live permanently, because she didn't like some Europeans' perception of Africans. To her, the classic European notions of Africa was that of a Dark Continent in every respect, with all the negative connotations that accompanied that phrase. She wasn't the type of person to compromise her cultural heritage. As far as she was concerned Nigeria was where she belonged. In Africa her status as royalty carried weight and respect.

It wasn't prejudice in England and Europe that bothered her. Prejudice, as far as she was concerned, was pre-judgement about something or someone known only from a distance. It was holding on to those ideas when personal experience should have taught someone that their previous judgement was wrong. That was racism.

Even though she held such strong views, she was quick to add that she had a lot of white friends, and many were more genuine and trustworthy than some black people, especially some Nigerians. She was happy enough with her English friends and the life-style and enjoyed living in England. That, as far as she was concerned, compensated for now at least for a whole lot of things she was missing by not living in Nigeria.

After dinner, no one talked about the previous night's party and Michael wondered whether Barbara knew Mr Anastasia, or any of Danny's associates.

The conversation ended abruptly when the telephone rang. Barbara answered it with a sense of urgency, as if she had expected the call. She asked to be excused, got dressed, said her goodbyes and was chauffeur driven away.

Shortly after that, Danny made a phone call and arranged a meeting with someone called Phidias who would be working with Michael.

A week later they drove to the Saints and Sinners Café in Broad Street, Birmingham City centre, to meet Phidias.

The Saints and Sinners was a strange but interesting place. It was a drop in joint for hippies and flower people, those looking for kicks, marijuana and other drugs. There were transvestites, some more than six feet tall, wearing size ten and eleven shoes and doing their vain best to look feminine. It was also a place where some people just came for a coffee and a chat. Everyone was cool and made welcome.

Phidias arrived on time. He was about the same age as Michael and Danny greeted him warmly, introduced Michael, and went to order coffee for all three of them. Michael and Phidius were about to take seats at a table, when there was the screech of tyres, the sound of a car door being slammed and a woman's scream. Through the café's window, a girl could be seen lying on the pavement. She had somehow fallen out of the car in which her boyfriend was motionless at the wheel, another man holding a knife at his windpipe.

Everyone rushed out to find out what was happening. It was almost dusk and the street lights had just come on. The light from the nearest lamp post reflected into the car and they could see blood running down the shirt of the boy with the knife at his throat.

Within no time at all there was the sound of sirens and two police cars arrived at the scene. The man with the knife was disarmed, bundled into a police car and taken away. An ambulance took the wounded boyfriend to the hospital. Whatever the cause of the near fatal tragedy to which they had been inadvertent witnesses, Danny, Michael and Phidias left the café without even drinking their coffee.

As they drove away, Michael was wondering how many more surprises were in store for him. In just over a week in Birmingham, he had seen, heard, and witnessed things that took some people a lifetime to experience.

Without any discussion they now drove to the Garden House Hotel, near the Rainbow Casino, on Hagley Road, and took a seat in a quiet corner of the hotel lounge. Phidias had a calm, likeable personality. He described himself as an out of work actor, now working for Danny.

It was a pleasant surprise for Michael to meet someone through Danny who was only five foot six inches tall. Nor was there anything in his persona that suggested aggression, unlike Danny's other associates. He wasted no time telling Michael about the kind of work he would be doing and explained that speed and coordination were the necessary talents.

Michael didn't have a problem with that. He was a boxer with natural fitness and coordination and he couldn't imagine that learning to spray cars would take him very long. He wasn't told where the spraying was to take place but Phidias arranged to meet him on Broad Street, the next evening. From there he would be taken to his first night's work.

He had committed himself, motivated by the desire to earn quick and easy money.

Later that night, he lay in bed contemplating his decision. Suddenly everything didn't seem so straight forward. He had only come to Birmingham to see an old friend and enjoy a weekend party. Instead, he was now entrenched in a new situation, without knowing the full story. He was beginning to wonder whether the excessive weekend partying and alcohol had clouded his reasoning.

He tried to dismiss all the intruding thoughts and to go with the flow, at least for the time being. Just then his thoughts were interrupted by the sound of a police siren in the distance, soon fading from earshot. He felt the tension of the moment and imagined the fear of living in the heart of a city, where life could sometimes be unpredictable. He was already aware of the beating heart of the city he didn't fully understand and that like everyone else he'd allowed himself to be caught up in the wheel of circumstances which included his own fears for tomorrow, the next day, and the next.

CHAPTER NINE

Danny drove Michael to the city centre to meet Phidias, to begin his first night's work.

Phidias was much the same as the first time they met. He was calm, and pleasant but didn't seem to be in any mood for conversation. It was as if he was focussing on the job ahead, or something else was also on his mind.

Michael was also feeling tense as he reflected on the events since he had arrived in Birmingham - Danny's life style, his front line experience, the surprise party, Mr Anastasia, and all the people he met, kept coming to the surface of his mind. He was beginning to wonder what he had let himself in for. But then again, thoughts of the money he would make surfaced. Somehow, the unconscious fear of the unexpected, and the desire for money, made it all…interesting. He was caught up between curiosity, fear, and that desire for the money.

Phidias drove them through back streets and eventually onto a well-hidden industrial estate. They arrived at about nine pm, passing other units with locked doors but the sound of activity going on inside them. It seemed a world apart from what was going on in the rest of the city.

At their destination Phidias rang the bell and the gate shutters were lifted by a not too friendly looking heavyweight who looked like someone wanted by the police. His greeting was a kind of groan that hardly equated with any word resembling *Hello*. He didn't even make eye contact with Michael or Phidias. It was an atmosphere which gave the impression that, at any moment, something unexpected could happen.

There was a partition in the middle of the garage hiding everything behind it from view. Michael could hear muffled pounding coming from behind it. He followed Phidias through to the work area. There was another heavy weight, nearly the same size as the one who had opened the shutters. His face was even more unfriendly and intimidating.

Three cars lay behind the partition - a Mercedes, a Jensen Interceptor and an Aston Martin. Phidias gave Michael a pair of overalls and explained what he had to do, while demonstrating on an old car in another corner of the garage. The three cars had to be painted different colours and must be finished within two weeks. Michael kept his mind focussed on the things Phidias was showing him, to try and learn as fast as possible but he could tell Phidias was nervous. Despite a calm, outward persona, Michael could sense discomfort. He himself wasn't too comfortable either in the tense atmosphere. The heavy weights worked in silence and finished about two hours later. They didn't bother to say goodbye when they left. Michael hoped he wouldn't see them again.

Apart from instructions about what to do, Phidias said little while they worked. Michael kept asking himself, what he was doing in a place like this with these strange people. He quickly answered the question in his own mind - *tax-free money.*

They worked throughout the night, stopping only once for a short break.

As far as Michael was concerned, everything was as clear as mud, but he didn't ask any questions. He guessed that the cars were to be sold abroad but had no interest in knowing any more. Knowledge could well be dangerous. He was there simply to earn as much as he could in the shortest possible time, spraying cars.

Days went by; then weeks. He settled into the work and was enjoying living in luxury with Danny and Barbara. More importantly, he was earning and saving the kind of money he had never dreamed possible. He sometimes wondered why he was being paid so much money; but didn't ask questions. He phoned Cynthia weekly, but never once discussed the kind of work he was doing. Now working with greater speed and efficiency, he thought he was doing a good job because Phidias never complained or scrutinised anything he did. He was always paid by Danny on a Friday and had never once had to ask for his money. They were still socialising occasionally, but he worked nights and slept during the day while Danny was largely conducting whatever business he did during daylight hours. They didn't see a lot of each other anymore except on a Saturday. Occasionally they would go to a weekend party. Michael felt they were drifting apart, but that didn't worry him too much. Spraying cars was much more tiring than he thought but his focus was on making money and heading back to London. Sometimes he would collect as much as £200 with bonuses for getting the job done quickly. It was a small fortune, compared to the average wage. He was also glad to be out of sight of Danny's associates. He kept his mind on what he was doing and collected the money.

After a few months, he was spraying all kinds of cars with far greater proficiency and had saved more than £2,000. He was now contemplating leaving in a few more weeks.. He hadn't seen Cynthia for a long time and was becoming home-sick, in spite of all the comforts he was enjoying at Danny's house.

The last time they spoke, Danny told him he had a very important job he wanted him to do and that he would be well paid for it. He didn't say what the job was, or when. Michael wasn't as keen any more. He had earned enough money to give Cynthia and himself a good start when they returned to Jamaica, and was ready to quit.

Barbara and Danny went abroad occasionally, for a few days. That meant he was in the house alone. He didn't mind that. It gave him time to think and he had space and all the comfort he had become accustomed to. However, the more he thought, the more he began to feel isolated and was longing now for Cynthia's company.

Early one morning when he finished working, he came home to find Danny in the lounge, drinking and looking as if he hadn't slept all night. His friend's face bore a worried look, as if he was under a lot of pressure. They sat in the lounge, drinking coffee and liquor and he was about to tell Danny he was thinking of going back to London at the end of the month when Danny said: 'You look like you need a holiday, Mike.'

Michael thought he was trying to tell him to quit. It seemed he was being encouraged to go and put the money he had saved to good use.

'Yea, as soon as I get back to London, I'm taking Cynthia on holiday. Somewhere nice for a week. Maybe it's time to see my island in the sun.'

'No, man. I mean, how would you like a holiday abroad in Europe. Germany, for example - a working holiday?'

'What's this all about, Danny? A working holiday?'

'A job in Berlin, man, just one week.'

'But I don't speak German.'

'You won't have to. You'll be dressed in uniform and driving a passenger who speaks perfects German. Money is good as well.'

'Don't bullshit me, Danny. What's this all about?'

Danny took a deep breath, got off his chair and started pacing the floor. 'Remember the blue Mercedes you sprayed a few weeks ago?'

'Yea.'

'It's fully paid for by one of our best customers and the guy who was supposed to take it abroad got into trouble. We need someone who looks the part, is intelligent, and has no police record.'

'Why not use a white man?'

'We can't take the chance and use the wrong person. Sometimes that's bad for business. Some of the guys who work with us have police records.'

'I couldn't have guessed,' was the response, with a touch of sarcasm.

Danny kept pacing the floor, waiting for an answer. Michael wasn't quite sure what to say.

'Listen, Danny, I'm grateful as hell that you got me this job, and I like the money. But I feel I'm getting deeper in shit, man. Of course I love the money and the life-style since I've been here. But you never told me that this operation was illegal when I started. If I knew I was going to be spraying stolen cars I never would have got involved. You told me nothing about the risks and I'm supposed to be a friend. As far as I'm concerned, you've thrown our friendship out of the window.'

'I was going to tell you everything as soon as the time was right, man.'

'Well you've taking your time. I've been living in your house for months now and you said nothing to me about any underground activities. And you're asking me to stick my neck out again. Anything could have happened to me over the past few months. No one knows where I'm working, what I'm doing, who I'm working with - not even Cynthia.'

'Believe me, brother, man, I'm grateful you've helped me out and you're doing a good job. But this time I really need your help. I'm in a tricky situation. I'll explain it all when you get back.'

'Back from where? As far as I'm concerned, I'm finished right now.' He was angry enough now to take the next train back to London.

'I've got a lot of money tied up with these people and I can't afford to let them down. I know I can trust you, man.'

'Yea, but can I trust you? I don't really want to know your business, but from day one, you should have told me about the risks. You might be used to all this underworld, cloak and dagger activity, but I'm not. And even though I don't mind earning money or getting rich, I don't want to die trying. What did you get yourself mixed up in, Danny?

You're running with gangsters and some people that look like hit men and you've drag me right in the middle of it all.'

'I'm sorry, man, I'll make it up to you.'

'Tell me this, Danny, who owns the car, and who is the passenger?'

'The car belongs to an English aristocrat who is out of the country for a while. The passenger you're carrying is East German. You've got to drive him to Berlin.'

'What? Do you think I'm fucking crazy to carry some foreigner I don't know? It's bad enough getting caught with an aristocrat's car. I don't want to get involved with no cloak and dagger operation with some East German. Jesus Christ, man, this is serious shit. Haven't you heard? There's a cold war going on and Berlin is a hot spot, full of spies and people dying every day. Don't you watch television and see how many people die every month, clinging to the Berlin wall, shot to pieces?'

'Relax, everything's cool. All his papers are in order and there's no risk to you. Brother, man, I've got a lot of money tied up in this business and with these people. I'm asking you as a personal favour. I'll buy you some shares when you get back.'

'Forget the shares, man. My safety is worth more than money. I need time to think. There's another thing you're overlooking. I'm a black man. As you probably know, black people aren't all that popular in Berlin.'

'No need to worry, man. Chauffeuring is a normal black man's job. No one will take any notice of you.'

The fact that Danny had done him a favour by giving him a well-paid job and tax free money, played on Michael's mind. Although he felt he had to repay Danny for his kindness, he had serious reservations. He didn't want to repay Danny by putting his life at risk, no matter how much gratitude he owed him. He got off his chair, looked out of the window, trying to think what to say or do. He had taken a chance before and so far was still in one piece but he didn't want to push his luck any further. Unfortunately, loyalty to Danny and money were again occupying his mind. He took a deep breath, looked at Danny and said, 'OK, I'll do it, depending on what you're paying me.'

Danny threw his arms around him. 'Don't worry about money, man. You get some money right now, up front, the rest when you get back.'

As Danny embraced him, Michael had the feeling he was behaving like a businessman who had just clinched a deal, rather than a genuine friend who wanted help. He wasn't sure how much trust and confidence he should put in him anymore. Suddenly he didn't feel like a friend but rather like someone being used.

'Keep cool, man. All you've got to do is drive the car to Berlin. When you get there, drop off your passenger, leave the car in a car park and put the keys in the glove compartment. Your hotel and flight will be paid for until you're ready to come home. You can spend a whole week or more, enjoying yourself, if you want to. It's as easy as that. Let's have another drink.'

'At nine o'clock in the morning?

'What the hell, we've had liquor early in the morning before.'

Danny poured two large glasses of brandy and toasted their future health and success. Michael wasn't all that confident about that, but at least the atmosphere became more relaxed and tensions were set aside for the moment. Still at the back of Michael's mind was the reality of the situation. This was more risky than spraying stolen cars. As soon as this trip was over, he would say farewell to Danny and England and be on his way to Jamaica, with Cynthia.

Danny opened his brief case and handed him £500. 'There'll be another £500 when you get back. You can buy as many Fräuleins as you want when you're in Berlin. I hear that German women are mad about black men, especially Jamaican men. You might even get a chance to see the Berlin Wall and Check Point Charlie, the border crossing between East and West Berlin.'

'I'm not interested in women, Danny. I've got Cynthia. And as for the Berlin Wall, I won't take too much pleasure in seeing it. It's got too many bad memories for a lot of people and their families according to what I hear. I'm just going to do the job you're paying me a lot of money for.'

'You're a brother and I'd like you to earn some real money. That's your destiny and mine, man.'

'That may be true for you Danny, but as soon as I get back from Berlin, it's over. I'm finished after this, no matter what you say or do.'

He said it with conviction, without showing anxiety, anger or fear.

Deep down inside he knew their so called friendship was at an end even the strength of the brandy and coffee was taking away some of his concerns.

'If you're questioned along the way, all you know is that you were hired as a chauffeur. Your passenger will do the talking. I'll arrange for you to pick up the car and the passenger in London.'

'How did you get mixed up with all this, Danny?'

'Brother, man, you worry too much. As soon as you get back I'll tell you the whole story.'

'I'm finished, man, whatever you say. I've been living in your house for months and you haven't told me anything. Why should I believe you now?'

Danny didn't want to end the relationship and Michael could see that he was feeling guilty for not sharing information from the first day he arrived in Birmingham. What started as a weekend visit, had become a money-making venture, which was now getting out of hand. He thought about INTERPOL and how they would probably nail him to the Berlin Wall because of his own greed and stupidity.

It wasn't normal for a black man to be driving an upmarket, stolen aristocrat's car and carrying a sinister passenger to Berlin. Michael couldn't help thinking that, if something went wrong, he was unlikely to see the strip of sun-baked island in the Caribbean called Jamaica ever again. He thought about how right his mother was when she said that *money was the root of all evil.* Worse, he had blurred the lines where courage ends and stupidity begins. He wondered whether he had been given horse manure for brains when he was born. That was the thought that lingered in his mind, as he got dressed and prepared to take the train to London.

Danny drove him to the station. On their way, there were spells of silence, moments it seemed, when both were reflecting. It was a kind of parting mood, with things weighing heavily on both minds. Most of Michael's focus was on reaching London and seeing Cynthia. During the short journey, there were also moments when it seemed tension could be pushed aside for old time sake. But those moments were imposters.

The sky was overcast and bleak; the air damp. Factory smoke, coke and coal fumes from surrounding houses and factories, created a macabre atmosphere. Gone was the warm weather that had greeted him when he first arrived in Birmingham. Instead, everything seemed to be under a heavy cloud.

As the train left the station and Danny waved him goodbye, he felt a sense of relief as he waved back.

The train belched its own mixture of fumes, adding to the pollution. Soon, Danny disappeared from view.

CHAPTER TEN

The young boy sitting opposite Michael on the train, kept sticking out his tongue and making faces.

His mother was too busy reading the fashion magazine to notice him climbing onto the back of the seat, threatening to fall on his head. She would occasionally scold him but then she let him carry on with his mischief, to the annoyance of other passengers.

Michael was looking out of the window at the small towns and villages rushing by, contemplating, his thoughts entangled with doubts, uncertainty and apprehension. He felt as if he was hanging over a precipice, driven there by the desire for money and a better future. He was trying to think of a way out when it dawned on him that all he had to do was give the money back to Danny and tell him he had changed his mind about the trip to Berlin. Come to think of it, he didn't even have to give back the money he had up front.

He soon reasoned that that kind of thinking was probably the worst thought he had had all day. To be a future practising lawyer required integrity. Not that integrity had played any part when he was working and earning money spraying stolen cars.

More worrying was another consequence. When he remembered the characters he met, Billy, Frank, Shaven-Head, Mr Anastasia and his bodyguards, he had to think carefully what not to do. It wouldn't be hard for them to arrange his permanent departure from his present life, he thought.

Returning the money Danny gave him up front was the best option, if he decided not to drive his passenger to Berlin.

As the train neared London, he became eager to see Cynthia, to hold her close and feel the warmth of her breath close to him. He just wanted to push all other thoughts to the back of his mind. In a few days he would be on the long drive to Berlin.

Cynthia rushed towards the front door as soon as she heard the key in the lock. Indoors, they held each other closely for a long time. All his fears drifted away as they embraced. He felt as if a great burden had been lifted from his shoulders, at least for the time being. Gone were the anxieties of the past months and thoughts about the task ahead. None of these now occupied any portion of his mind.

They went out that evening and enjoyed the best of everything. He didn't mention anything about going to Berlin in a few days' time, until the end of the evening when they returned home. She wasn't pleased, but when he explained everything to her and showed her the money he had saved while working for Danny, she became more relaxed. He didn't talk about the kind of work he had done in Birmingham either or why he was going to Berlin. All she knew was that he was driving a passenger and would be back in about a week.

The following day they went to the bank and deposited his money.

The car he was driving to Berlin was locked away in a garage in Camberwell Green. He collected it under the cover of darkness, as arranged. Dressed in a chauffeur's uniform, he made sure he had his passport and everything else needed for the journey.

He collected his passenger as also arranged. Dressed in a bowler hat and dark pin-striped-suit, the man carried an air of arrogance making himself comfortable in the back seat of the Mercedes after curtly introducing himself.

Michael didn't like him from the moment they met. Stone-faced, his attempted smile looked so false. Michael wondered why he even bothered. He looked very distinguished, but obviously believed he was superior to everyone around him. There was an aristocratic air about him, a kind of attitude that could easily annoy anyone whose path he crossed. To Michael, he looked like someone from the Boris Karloff era, with only a touch of modernity.

The note in the envelope that Danny had given him, said that his passenger's name was Pickersgill. It didn't sound a Germanic name but it suited his persona. He looked at Michael as if he was far inferior to him, someone from whom he expected total obedience and compliance. When he introduced himself, he made sure he said his name with careful emphasis, delivered slowly, as if to say *make sure you know who you are talking to*. Michael wasn't impressed or worried about what he thought about himself. All he was interested in was delivering him to Berlin, as he had promised Danny he would. He watched Pickersgill in his rear view mirror as he composed himself and prepared for the journey. When the man was ready, he said one word, 'Drive.'

They were on their way.

When the customs officer collected his passport at Dover, Michael looked straight-ahead, avoiding eye contact, like an obedient chauffeur should. He was behaving like someone with his mind on the job. His passenger was treated with the utmost courtesy and respect, as if he was some kind of celebrity but the trip across the channel was un-eventful. Apart from looks of curiosity and the occasional whispers, obviously referring to his colour, everything seemed normal.

Shortly after arriving in Hamburg, he discovered that there are few thrills to compare with driving along the Autobahn at high speed, in a high performance car. When he accelerated and felt the power of the engine, he tried to overtake everything, for sheer pleasure and to meet his deadline. Driving on roads where there were no speed limits was a wonderful feeling and his adrenalin was flowing. He was in command of a beautiful machine; excited. The whole experience was beginning to feel like an ego trip. Even Pickersgill, his suit still uncreased, Brylcreem in his hair, was under his control now. It was a good feeling.

He began to imagine how those who usually controlled others must feel. Power, the ability to control circumstances, exert force and determine outcomes, was a great tool. He was deep in focus, doing ninety miles an hour and enjoying the moment.

The sudden sound of a siren interrupted his thoughts. It startled him, but the police car flashed past and in a moment was gone. The surprise brought back reality. He had almost forgotten the seriousness of his `situation and suddenly remembered he wasn't on a merry go round ride in a fair ground. He was driving a probably stolen car, in a foreign country, at high speed and carrying a passenger he had only met a few hours earlier. Even worse, he was a black man, in a country characterised for him by Hitler's refusal to shake hands with four times Olympian, Jesse Owens at the 1936 Berlin Olympics.

'Pull over at the next petrol station, will you?'

He couldn't believe his ears. Pickersgill had actually used a complete sentence, instead of a single word command. It even sounded like a request rather than an order. For the first time, he also heard Pickersgill with a German accent as the car window was lowered and he spoke to the petrol pump attendant, in German. 'Macht es voll, bitte.' His accent was perfect, similar to the German newscaster's accent Michael had been hearing on the radio as they drove along. There wasn't the least trace of English now in that voice which took Michael by surprise. When he first met Pickersgill, with his air of arrogance and aristocracy, he couldn't have imagined that he might be someone else entirely.

The petrol attendant stared at Michael and said: 'Hallo. 'He imitated the accent and returned the greeting. He probably thought Michael was an African driving his colonial master to some exotic place. He even waved them good-bye as they drove away.

An hour after they had left the petrol station, they stopped at a motorway restaurant. Pickersgill took off his hat and gloves, went inside and after fifteen minutes, returned with two neatly wrapped packages. One contained food, the other beers. They ate Wurst und Kartoffelsalat in silence and drank their beers listening to an American baseball commentary on, on the radio.

Michael's curiosity finally got the better of him, just before they finished eating. 'Mr Pickersgill?'

'Yes, what is it?

'How comes your German and English are so perfect?'

'You're paid to drive me; not to ask questions.'

'I know that, but I'd be much happier if I knew exactly who I was driving around.'

'I just told you. You're paid to drive, not to interrogate me.'

'I bet some other people would like to ask you a few questions.'

Pickersgill slowly put the rest of his sausage and potato salad in its container and reached under his seat. When Michael saw the black muzzle of the gun, the mayonnaise in his mouth suddenly tasted like mud. He didn't know whether to swallow or spit it out. It was like taking a sip of piping hot black coffee and losing control of all the muscles in your mouth that would help make a decision about what to do. He just opened his mouth and the food fell out.

Pickersgill's mood had suddenly switched to one of ice-cold anger. 'This, Mr nosey Parker, is a forty-five. If you keep asking questions and making remarks like that, you will see the flames coming from the muzzle, directly, and feel the effects of one or two bullets. And in case you didn't notice, it has a silencer as well. So, if you don't keep your mouth shut from now on, or mess things up in Berlin, you'll never get back to England alive. That's a promise. Now drive, we're running late.'

Michael started the car and pulled out onto the autobahn, his nerves now on edge. The front of his trousers was wet from the beer he spilled when Pickersgill pulled out his gun. The moment of agonising fright lingered as he kept his mind focussed on the road ahead while trying to think. The situation was much more dangerous than he had realised.

From now on he was going to keep his mouth shut and make sure he did nothing to upset his passenger. He would only speak if spoken to, or if he had something to say that wouldn't put him at risk.

He was again in the middle of free flowing traffic, whizzing past high-speed cars, with a sense of urgency and a renewed awareness of the danger he was in.

Before long they were on the outskirts of Berlin.

Pickersgill had said very little since their confrontation apart from occasionally giving directions. He had demonstrated that he was a serious contender for dishing out violence if he had to and now that he had nearly reached his destination, Michael was worried that he might decide Michael had outlived his usefulness. He tried to remain calm, but deep down he was becoming angrier with Danny for putting him in this predicament.

Years after the war ended, the Germans were still in the process of clearing and demolishing dilapidated 1buildings. They drove around for some time but Michael guessed Pickersgill knew his way around the city and was merely marking time but he never disclosed any of his intentions.

'Turn next left and drive to the car park on the opposite side.'

Michael followed his instructions, nervously pondering what might happen next. He kept getting flashbacks of the first time he saw a gun on top of the wardrobe, in Trench Town, that experience now competing with the gun and the silencer Pickersgill introduced him to. The main difference was that this was real danger. He could remember the rage in Pickersgill's eyes as he spoke and was fully aware that this was a life and death situation.

'Drop me at the next corner, by the car park, drive into the car park and park the car. Wait for twenty minutes. Then leave the keys in the glove compartment and you can go. And don't forget, you've never met me. If you open your mouth while you are in Berlin, or when you get back to England, your life won't be worth anything. I've got friends everywhere.'

Pickersgill put his bowler hat on, took the gun from under the seat and put it in his briefcase. He slammed the car door and walked away, using his umbrella as a walking cane.

Michael listened to the footsteps until they were out of earshot. Then he did exactly as Pickersgill had instructed and put the keys in the glove compartment.

Another car pulled into the car park so he sat in the car and waited. The couple in the other car eventually left and drove away. That caused him more suspicion and additional anxiety. He tried to figure out why someone would drive into a car park and then drive away after a few minutes. Winter was setting in and it was almost dark.

After twenty minutes he got out and walked towards the bright lights along the main street towards Charlottenburg. He headed for the city centre where he could feel more secure, mingling with city people who were going about their business. His motorway ordeal with Pickersgill was still fresh in his mind.

He passed the old cathedral that was bombed during the war and stood on the edge of the pavement for a moment, to collect his thoughts. Just then he saw a taxi coming and waved it down. The driver pulled up beside him and he showed him the name of the hotel he had written on a piece of paper.

The driver, obviously thinking he was an American, told him in English to climb in. 'You are American soldier?'

'No, British tourist, on holiday.'

'English?'

'No! Jamaican living in England.'

'Ach so.'

'Your English is very good,' said Michael, trying to make conversation.

'I don't speak very good English but I speak American.'

The taxi driver was obviously proud of his pseudo American accent and began to tell Michael about some of the places to go for nightlife in the American Sector. He wrote them down, but all he wanted to do was to reach the hotel and unwind. The tiredness and fatigue from driving and his experience with Pickersgill, was beginning to affect him.

Reaching the hotel, he paid the taxi driver and settled into his room before telephoning Danny. He was angry and Danny felt the weight of his tongue as he hurled abuse at him. The last thing he had expected was to be put in a situation where he had a gun pointed at him.

Danny apologised and said he would explain everything when he got back to England, and that he would make it up to him with extra money. But Michael didn't want apologies, promises or even money for that kind of experience. He slammed the phone down in anger without even saying goodbye and climbed into bed, hoping sleep would erase the day's traumatic experience from his mind. He tried to eliminate the thoughts of fear, pain and worry as he struggled to fall asleep. But sleep wouldn't come.

He turned on the radio by his bedside. It was already on the American forces network. He listened to the sound of Duke Ellington's big band and tried to submerge himself in the music; to push everything to the back of his mind but he kept seeing Pickersgill's face and remembering the fear he had felt looking down the barrel of the gun.

As he lay there sleepless, all the people he met from the first day he arrived in Birmingham, kept haunting him like ghosts from the past. In the middle of them all was Danny. He couldn't trust him anymore. As far as he was concerned, all he cared about now was his own survival and Cynthia. Nothing else.

CHAPTER ELEVEN

After a restless night in the hotel, he got dressed early and went for breakfast. While he ate he tried to figure out how to spend the day. He decided to find another hotel. Danny knew where he was staying and it was more than likely that Pickersgill, Mr. Anastasia, and some of their strong arm men had the same information. As far as he was concerned he had done the job Danny asked him to do. His time was now his own.

He wasn't quite sure where to go, but after breakfast, he packed his bags and checked out. There was a taxi outside the hotel and he climbed in, hoping the driver could speak English.

The man's English wasn't as good as the driver he had met the previous day but it was more than enough to communicate. The driver took him on a tour of the city, pointing out famous landmarks. They passed Tempel Hof Airport, then on to an isolated hotel the other side of Schoenberg.

He saw a group of black American soldiers on his way and felt more comfortable to know that he wasn't the only black man around. The taxi parked outside the hotel and the driver tried to give him as much information as he could about where to go.

'Zee American sector is ein sehr schoner ort, I mean, a very nice place. Tonight you should go to the *International Club* or *Birdland*. You zee plenty pretty girls zere. Did you know zey named *Birdland* after Charlie Parker?' he continued, pleased with his language skills and his knowledge about nightlife in the American sector. Michael was more impressed to know that he had heard of the celebrated, alto saxophone player. He smiled, gave the man a large tip and thanked him for the information.

Later he took another taxi to the heart of the city, bought a camera and did some sightseeing. He stayed out nearly all day and didn't spend any more time worrying. As far as he was concerned, he had put some distance between himself and Pickersgill. He couldn't think of any reason why Pickersgill or anyone else would want to keep an eye on him now. Back at the hotel he telephoned Cynthia to let her know he was fine but they got disconnected during the conversation. He phoned Danny's house but there was no answer.

In the evening he took a taxi from outside his hotel. It dropped him at the Birdland Club in Schoenberg. It was a nightspot, mainly used by black American service men but some whites in uniform were hanging around outside. As he walked towards the entrance, he could hear a band playing the James Brown song: 'It's A Man's World'.

He went inside and shortly after, a six-piece band came on stage with a lead singer who sounded like Otis Reading. The club was packed. Alcohol was flowing, bottles of spirits and wine on every table and nearly everyone had a glass in their hand. It was the end of the month when American GIs were paid. People were dancing, having a good time. He tried to adjust to the atmosphere. With money in his pocket, he didn't feel out of place.

She walked towards him as he neared the bar. Her intense gaze conveyed a message that said: the beginning of a conversation is imminent. Her mini-skirt didn't leave very much to the imagination and she smelt as if she just had a bath in Chanel No.5. He stopped and returned her fixed gaze with a friendly smile. It wasn't a smile that extended an invitation or submission - more of a courtesy smile, with quiet admiration. After all it hadn't been sexual motives which drew him out of his hotel room.

She didn't hesitate. 'You're new round here, aren't you?' Delivered with an inviting smile, trying to be sensual and sophisticated at the same time. She had a pseudo American accent but he could tell she was unmistakably German. She was also drunk.

'Yea,' he said, looking straight in her eyes, eyes that were glazed by too much alcohol.

'Would you like a drink? 'she purred, as she took his arm and led him towards the bar. He didn't refuse the invitation or her company. A stranger in a strange place, he reasoned any kind of hospitality was acceptable. His German was poor, so anyone who could speak German and English would be a good person to have around.

Without even asking him what he wanted to drink, she ordered double bourbon and ice, twice.

'Are you American?'

'Jamaican.'

'Is that where the sexy music come from, you know, calypso, ska and reggae?'

'That's right,'

She put her arms around his waist, held him tightly and called out to the bartender again.

'Bartender, where are those drinks for me and my Jamaican man?' She sounded as if she had watched some old Hollywood movie and wanted to impress him with her acting skills. She seemed proud she was with a Jamaican, knowing that Jamaicans had a reputation of one kind or another. He didn't raise any objection when she claimed he was her man. That wasn't a good enough reason to be impolite or abandon her, because he wasn't taking the encounter seriously.

The bartender brought the drinks and she ordered two more, even before they started drinking the first order. She drained her glass as if it was water, and finished the second with the same speed.

She talked for about ten minutes, without making sense, before staggering away to claim another man she called, Lattimer. He was wearing an American Air Force uniform. That was a welcome break for Michael. He was planning to get rid of her before but hadn't known how to go about it. He paid for the drinks she had ordered and then took a seat in a dimly lit corner of the club. It was a good vantage point. From there he watched the singer on stage as he belted out the words of: 'I Can't Get No Satisfaction', trying to imitate Otis Redding. From where he was sitting, he spotted a lone figure in another corner of the club. Although the club was dimly lit, he noticed she had a tall glass containing what might have been Martini. She was playing with the condensation on the side of the glass, looking bored, but reserved.

He couldn't stop himself and kept glancing over to where she was for some time and then got up and walked straight over to her, introduced himself and asked whether he could have a seat.

She was still toying with her glass as she answered. 'It doesn't cost anything to sit down.' Her response was mildly assertive, with no overt indication that she had any real interest in her new arrival. She was attractive and that more than compensated for what might at first be interpreted as a not overly sociable attitude. He guessed she was being defensive, maybe had a lot on her mind. Before he left his table, he had decided to start a conversation with her out of pure bravado.

He told her his name. She gave hers as 'Ingrid,' and before too long they were engaged in polite conversation. With his charismatic charm, he found the opportunity to inject some mild humour and it was if the brazen confidence of his approach, had taken her by surprise. He wasn't behaving like the typical Black American GI who had just received his monthly pay cheque and was looking for hot pleasure at any cost. She recognised that and began to relax in his company. It transpired that she was German and spoke fluent English, and French and she had worked in England for a few years.

He told her he was in Berlin on holiday, the same story he had told the taxi drivers. A stranger in an unknown city, he was happy to have a platonic relationship with someone, without ulterior motives.

She was out to enjoy herself and it was her first time in that part of the city. Also a stranger in town, it soon became clear that she was a loner and out of place in a nightclub, by herself. And hadn't appreciated that in a Cold War Zone, on pay night, GIs would be looking for more than just to dance the night away.

He had no expectations as they shared the evening together. They stayed at the Birdland until late into the night, even complimenting each other on their respective dance skills. She ended up driving him back to his hotel and they arrange to meet the following day.

Michael was eager to talk to Danny but it was too late to telephone him then so he tried early the following morning but no one answered. He decided to just enjoy the rest of his stay until it was time to board his pre-booked flight back to England. As soon as this mini holiday was over, he would spend a few months in England and book a flight to Jamaica, with Cynthia.

He couldn't help thinking that if Pickersgill had wanted him dead, there had been lots of opportunities on the Autobahn. He could have shot him at a lay-by or in the car park, using the silencer and no one would have heard. Obviously that wasn't part of the original plan. There must have been another reason why Pickersgill didn't want to drive himself to Berlin. Whatever the reason, it was all well planned. Another possibility was that Danny didn't know the whole story, although that was unlikely. He couldn't accept that reasoning either, and thought the best thing to do was to stay away from Charlottenburg until it was time to go back to England. Berlin was a big city and it would be hard to find anyone without a specific lead. That was his thinking. But in moments of danger or worry, all kinds of conflicting signals can surface. One thing he was certain about, was that he had no intention of contacting Danny for the rest of the money he was owed for doing the job. He didn't want to spend the rest of his time in Berlin locked away in his hotel room but nor did he want to risk running into Pickersgill. To venture out, he needed someone who could speak German as well as English and knew the city well.

Ingrid was ideal especially if he decided to spend most of his time in Schoenberg where there were lots of black American soldiers. He still had five days left in Berlin, and spending time in pleasant company was certainly one way to free him from some of his anxieties. He knew his situation was still precarious and safety first had to be his motto. Ingrid could be a good companion, an interpreter, as well as a guide around the city.

They met at the International Club as arranged and had a good evening together. Then she invited him home and it was an offer he couldn't refuse. They spent the night together at Ingrid's flat in the suburbs, without any kind of intimacy. Through the night they talked about aspects of their lives. He told her about his relationship with Cynthia, but avoided mentioned anything about Danny.

An artist by profession, Ingrid's flat was nicely decorated, with pictures hanging everywhere. There were copies of Leonardo Da Vinci's *Mona Lisa*, *The Madonna* by Raphael and a sketch by Picasso. More striking still was a copy of Cezanne's portrait of his wife. The last piece seemed to be a mirror image of part of Ingrid's psychological profile but she knew how to disguise her solitude and loneliness. There was no evidence in the flat that she had a man in her life; only that she had dedicated her time to her work.

Most of her personal work was filled with bright colours and intricate lines and spaces, almost to the point of being abstract. That was the impression Michael had of her work, an uninformed, subjective assessment, based on his limited knowledge of art. She tried to enlighten him about the motivation and driving force behind a painter's imagination, and her own work. Not that he understood most of what she was saying, from an aesthetic point of view but it certainly was a diversion from his experiences of recent days. He was relaxed and happy to know that, for the moment he had distanced himself from that negativity. He already felt light years away from the incidents of his recent past.

When he went back to his hotel the following day, he telephoned Danny who sounded anxious and told him to keep out of sight and take a different flight back to England. He didn't say why. The phone went dead. It was the last thing he wanted to hear. There were more alarm bells ringing in his head and his anxiety had returned. The relationship between him and Danny was over, as far as he was concerned but suddenly there was a new twist. The first question that came to him was, *What did I do to deserve this?* It was a question he had asked himself many times, after making bad decisions. He even remembered once, going to the bathroom and asking himself the same question as he looked in the mirror. For a moment he had thought he saw a reflection of six letters printed on his forehead, which read *STUPID*.

Because Danny didn't have time to explain what the problem was before they got cut off, Michael's new worry revolved around trying to work out what might be happening. All he could think of was that, he was getting buried deeper in the quagmire.

Shortly after they got disconnected, he telephoned Ingrid to ask if he could stay at her flat until it was time to get his flight back to England. She agreed and he packed his bags and waited for her to pick him up at the hotel. When she arrived she wanted to know why he had suddenly decided to leave the hotel. He told her he was missing her, feeling lonely and wanted to be with her. There was some truth in that, although it was far from the whole truth.

Ingrid took him on a tour of the city. She drove towards the Brandenburg Gate; passed Check Point Charlie, the border crossing from East Berlin to West Berlin. Michael knew there had been many tense incidents and confrontations there between American and Russian soldiers during the cold war. As they looked on from a distance, he realised there were probably many Germans there who detested the presence of foreign soldiers in their divided city. Many families had become separated during the building of the Berlin Wall. Barbed wire, Russian and East German soldiers with guns, at the crossing, gave very little hope to those in East Berlin wishing to unite with their families in the West. Many had risked and lost their lives, in an effort to reunite with one another. Thinking about the whole situation gave Michael a feeling of empathy for those who were trapped in the city. Danny had just told him to keep out of sight and not to take his return flight while Pickersgill had earlier warned him to keep his mouth shut. Something sinister was happening behind the scenes and he had no way of knowing what it was.

As they drove through the city, there were moments when his now overactive imagination started racing. He even imagined crossing to East Berlin on a day trip, just for the hell of it. He soon realised doing that would be well past crazy. People were trying to escape to the West and he was thinking of a day trip to East Berlin. It was a moment of confusion and madness that quickly passed.

Ingrid suggested they go to the edge of the Grunewald for a walk, to get away from city traffic and get a change of scenery. They arrived at the forested area, parked the car and walked on in companionable silence. However, it wasn't long before Ingrid noticed a worried look on Michael's face and asked what was wrong.

He just looked at her, smiled and told her everything was OK. He knew she didn't really believe him but he didn't want to tell her that he was mixed up with the underworld. Berlin was a city where suspicion, fear and espionage still existed more than twenty years after the Second World War had ended. It crossed Michael's mind that, if he wasn't careful and everything went very, very wrong, he could end up occupying a cold, clammy patch of German soil, forever.

If someone had said that to him months before, he might have said that was impossible, and a joke that was in bad taste. Now, this was a real situation on the brink of causing him serious alarm. Outwardly, he seemed calm, in control but below the surface he was busy trying to resolve the turmoil. His urgent wish was for Pickersgill to have long disappeared somewhere underground, along with the Mercedes.

The walk through the Grunewald took nearly an hour. That gave them enough time to talk about almost anything that came to mind. Ingrid began to ask questions, some of which he couldn't escape answering without blatantly lying. He told her part of the story, including his relationship with Danny and that he had driven Pickersgill to Berlin. Although he didn't lie he was economical with the truth. There was a sense of fear in his voice as he told her about the incident with the gun, on the autobahn.

His story now became a source of worry for her. She told him he should stay indoors, in her flat, till it was time to leave for England. He could see the sympathetic look in her eyes as he thanked her.

He was about to embrace her, when he remembered that Danny Knew Cynthia's address in London. He took Ingrid's hand and began to run towards the car.

His sudden change of mood startled her and she kept asking what was wrong. He told her that he must get to a telephone. They reached the car, drove to a telephone box and Ingrid dialled the operator to get connected to Cynthia's number. To his relief she answered immediately.

She wanted to know when he would be home.

He didn't bother to explain. 'Listen, Cynthia, I don't want you to worry or argue with me. Just do as I say. I'll explain everything later when I call you again. I want you to move in with your friend, Hyacinth, as soon as possible. Go to her house and stay there. Get in touch with Sweet Man, tell him what I've told you and ask him to keep an eye on everything. He'll know how to handle it. Don't stay in the flat any longer than you have to.'

'For God's sake, Michael, what's wrong? Where are you?'

'I'm in Berlin. I can't explain now, just do as I say.'

'I'm frightened Michael, someone keeps phoning here and as soon as I pick up the phone they hang up.'

'You know I love you, don't you?'

'And I love you too Michael, but I'm frightened.'

'Just do as I say, I'll explain later.'

Danny knew nothing about Hyacinth or where she lived so Michael hoped that Cynthia would be safe there. Hyacinth, a qualified nurse, was Cynthia's best friend. She lived in an exclusive part of London where she would be hard to find.

Ingrid was twisting with embarrassment overhearing the intimate conversation but he gave Cynthia Ingrid's telephone number and they said goodbye. Ingrid could see just how worried Michael was as he left the telephone box and she couldn't help herself. She threw her arms around his neck with affection. They could both feel the emotional intensity of their embrace. For the moment, he was caught up between two women, emotionally. He was in love with one and unsure what to feel for the other. At that moment, Ingrid's empathy was helping to soothe his emotional and psychological pain.

They arrived back at the flat, somewhat subdued by events but not deflated. So often in such moments, alcohol and intimacy can eject fear, worry and anxiety from the mind. So it was now. For those moments, a sensual, sexual encounter drove out the fear both now carried for the danger they were clearly in.

Cynthia phoned the following day to say that she had been able to move in with Hyacinth. She was very emotional and Sweet Man had to take the telephone from her. Michael told him in detail what he could remember, from the first day he arrived in Birmingham and asked him to try and find out what was happening. He knew Sweet Man must knew people in Birmingham, some from the underworld and would be able to get information about Danny and Mr. Anastasia.

Above all else he needed to know what was going on.

CHAPTER TWELVE

Michael lay in bed beside Ingrid, wondering what to do.

She was fast asleep, tired from sharing some of his anxieties throughout the day and making passionate love during the night. Now that he was back to reality, his mind was again in overdrive. He thought about walking up to a British Military Policeman and telling him the story of his life and about Pickersgill. That option was quickly dismissed.

Being black was only fashionable if you were a musician, entertainer or athlete. Even more so in Berlin. The Civil Rights Movement in America, the Black Panthers, black awareness and black pride, had stirred up further resentment of black people in America and as usual, how America treated black people was to some extent, reflected internationally. The phrase coined by James Brown: 'Say it loud, I'm black and I'm proud,' had served to inflame the status quo in America and the media and the legal machinery were unsympathetic. They were portraying black people as troublemakers, drug users and criminals and those who stood up for their rights - Angela Davis, Huey Newton, Bobby Seal and their like – were demonised.

These were the considerations in Michael's mind as he realised that it would be the height of stupidity to hand himself over to the British or to the American Military Police for safety. He wouldn't know where to start his story. He just couldn't think straight.

Just then, Ingrid turned over in bed, interrupting his moments but even the warmth of her body could not divert his attention from the seriousness of his situation. He had delivered part of his future into Danny's hands and was now haunted by fear. Even worse, he had been unfaithful to Cynthia. At the end of it all, if he was still alive, he would have to tell Cynthia. He had never lied to her before and planned not to in the future. Perhaps she wouldn't ask him whether he had had intimate relations with Ingrid and he needn't volunteer that information. If confronted he was prepared to admit his moment of weakness and ask forgiveness, if confronted by that situation but was philosophical enough to hope that some moments of his recent past would not be have to be resurrected when he returned home.

In spite of it all, he was getting used to life in Berlin. Five days had past and he had even managed to learn some German words. He phoned Cynthia daily. She knew he was living in Ingrid's flat. He tried to contact Danny but no one answered the telephone. Knowing that Cynthia was safe, he decided to try and enjoy the rest of his stay in Berlin and to spend another week with Ingrid before booking his return flight. He wanted to tour the city and take pictures with his newly bought camera.

Mentally he tried to trace his steps from the first time he had arrived in Berlin. He wanted to find where he had parked the Mercedes. He asked Ingrid to take him for a drive through Spandau and Charlottenburg and with her help, he retraced the car park. They stopped opposite and to his surprise, the Mercedes was still there. He couldn't believe his eyes. Everything became more intriguing. They sat and waited for nearly half an hour but nobody approached the Mercedes and nothing unusual happened.

They drove around the block a few times before deciding to head home. On the way, he wrestled with possible answers. Maybe the car was too hot and the person who was supposed to collect it had abandoned the idea. It could be that Pickersgill was the expensive commodity that had to be delivered to Berlin, and the Mercedes wasn't as important as Danny had made out.

Although reluctant to do so, he decided he had to try to contact

Danny again that evening. The telephone rang several times before Barbara answered. As usual, her voice was quietly dignified, but now there was an undercurrent of nervousness.

She said, 'Michael, Danny's been arrested and Frank's been shot dead in the city centre. The car you drove to Berlin is carrying gold bars in hidden compartments. It's part of Mr Pickersgill's wartime legacy. Some of the gold was stolen from people in concentration camps. He's wanted for war crimes.'

He listened as Barbara told him how Danny, Mr Anastasia and Pickersgill were working together. She talked for about ten minutes, but couldn't explain why Danny had told him not to take the pre-booked return flight. She said she was thinking of going back to Nigeria, because she was afraid. Before she hung up, Michael promised to call her the following day.

The next day when he phoned no one answered.

From spraying stolen cars, he had now got himself mixed up with a war criminal and stolen gold. He reasoned that no one would believe that he was an innocent victim who just earned some money by spraying cars. He didn't know whether to laugh or cry.

He put the phone down, staring at the wall, as if in a trance.

When Ingrid asked him what was wrong, it took him awhile before he could explain. He didn't even feel like talking. He had a lot of sympathy for Barbara and even Frank for losing his life. Any sympathy he had for Danny though was in a very small dose.

Cynthia's safety was more of his concern. Things had taken a wholly unexpected turn and it seemed Pickersgill's threats were far from idle threats. Bob Dylan's song: 'Knocking On Heaven's Door,' came into his mind like an ear worm which wouldn't quit. He had let loyalty to Danny and his desire for money, lead him down a dark alley and he didn't want to end up like Frank...or

Danny.

Ingrid poured a drink and went to the kitchen to prepare food. It gave him time to recover a little equanimity. He kept staring at the telephone, thinking what to do. They had made plans to go out the following day but he now considered that it was hardly a time for celebration. He tried to read between the lines of the things Barbara didn't say. It was beginning to become obvious that Danny must have known about the gold in the Mercedes and who Pickersgill really was which explained why he was offered so much money to chauffeur him to Berlin. He guessed that the fact the Mercedes was still there, meant something had gone terribly wrong. *It's also possible*, he thought, *that Barbara could have known all along what was going on.* She couldn't have given him all that information otherwise.

Reluctantly, he told Ingrid about the gold in the Mercedes. She was now part of the scenario and at risk, as long as he was around her. He started to think about her safety and decided to book his flight as soon as possible. Ingrid suggested they should go out, get drunk and forget about all their troubles for the evening. As they sat down to eat, his mind was doing somersaults, trying to figure out what to do.

They were eating in silence when Ingrid stopped and stared at him. She put her knife and fork on the edge of the plate and started laughing, uncontrollably.

'What's so funny?

'Think, Michael, Think?

'Think what?'

'Why don't we try and get that gold for ourselves?'

He stared at her. 'Are you crazy?'

'Why not, Michael? The car's been there for more than a week. If someone was coming to collect it they would have done it by now.'

'Pickersgill would kill us both.'

'Just think of the things you could do with four or five bars of that gold, Michael.'

'Don't you know history, Ingrid? Look how many people died in Africa, America, Australia, all over the world, trying to get gold.'

'True, but look at how many people are rich because of gold.'

'There are more dead ones than rich ones, and I'd rather be alive and poor. Tangling with the likes of Pickersgill and his kind of friends is a bad idea. I want to go back to that strip of island, called Jamaica, in one piece.'

'Would you take me with you? Oh no, I was only joking. I shouldn't have said that. I forgot about Cynthia.'

'It's OK, we can talk about it later,' was Michael's response, to soften her blushes.

She took up her knife and fork and started eating again, but with less enthusiasm. Perhaps she was really disappointed with him. After a few moments she said, 'We'll forget all about the gold then,' but her tone was sulky.

'Let me think about this, Ingrid.'

She smiled again then, happy to know he hadn't totally abandoned the idea.

CHAPTER THIRTEEN

The Café Kai'z, a well-known nightspot in the heart of Berlin, was their destination for the evening. Exclusively German, as Ingrid told him before they left home. Michael was looking forward to the reaction he would get when they walk through the door together. Not that he cared what anyone would think.

He was right though. They were the focus of attention as they walked in, Ingrid clinging to his arm. He spotted raised eyebrows. He wasn't sure if they were surprised or were admiring him for his audacity.

The place was a large nightclub rather than a café and was packed with well-dressed Germans of all ages. The band on stage was playing what sounded like a mixture between a fox trot and German martial music. Nearly everyone seemed in high spirits and the tables were littered with schnapps glasses and beer bottles.

They stood by the edge of the dance floor and looked around, searching for a comfortable seat. They didn't know what to expect, but Michael was determined to take everything in his stride as if he was another Berliner. Spotting an empty table, they crossed the dance floor, Michael wishing he could hear some black music with fire, rhythm and sensuality, similar to what was happening in Schoenberg, in the American sector. The music of the Café Kai'z was a total contrast to the free-wheeling jazz and soul sounds they'd enjoyed at International and at Birdland. The music here seemed more a reflection of the nineteen thirties and forties as if German attitudes and tastes had stood still for twenty years. It was as if nothing had changed musically, for them.

Michael said nothing to Ingrid. There was no point in complaining. He was prepared to tolerate and enjoy the night, whatever the situation. Everyone seemed to be having fun after all. Their laughter and loud conversation suggested they were already loaded with alcohol.

Approaching their empty table, they were greeted with friendly, hallos and more laughter. They took their seats and ordered drinks. Michael looked around to see if there was another black face, but there were none. It was worse than looking for a McDonalds Franchise in Antarctica. He guessed many Germans thought him privileged to be in the Cafe Kai'z. Subconsciously it gave him a feeling of importance, because he was a novelty. Some Germans, no doubt, were still passionate Nazis and were probably wondering what the hell a black man was doing in their night club, with a white German woman but he didn't care what anyone was thinking.

Before long, the evening began to turn out better than he had expected. German schnapps and beer saw to that. He even managed to dance some semblance of fox trot and quickstep. For posterity, occasionally he would throw in a few James Brown dance moves to demonstrate his dexterity on the dance floor. They made friends with the people at the next table who thought he was an American soldier. When he told them he was on holiday from England, they tried to teach him German. The more he drank, the more his German improved. Well, he was convinced it did even if all he added was another ten or so more words to the two dozen Ingrid had taught him.

A few hours later, his head was swirling and he felt relieved when Ingrid suggested it was time to go home. He had had more than enough to drink and was unsteady on his feet but they exchanged addresses with the people at the next table and said 'Good night,' before they left.

It was well past midnight.

Snow had fallen while they were in the warm, secure haven of the Café Kai'z. There was a degree of wind chill too and the cold instantly rushed to their lungs. They quickened their steps and staggered through the snow towards the Volkswagen they had left in a side street.

Ingrid was about to open the door, when two men dressed in black overcoats, came out of the shadows. One of them said, 'Put your hands on top of the car where we can see them. Don't move or make a sound.'

In his drunken state, Michael thought he was dreaming but the nightmare was only too real. He knew instantly the voice belonged to Pickersgill and that the man was deadly serious. The gun pointed at him for a second time attested to that even if the voice itself was calmy matter of fact. He knew Pickersgill wasn't bluffing. Frank's recent death in mind, he did exactly as Pickersgill had ordered and told Ingrid to do the same.

Pickersgill came closer, gun at the ready. It looked like the same gun he had produced when they were on the autobahn but it could have been a water pistol for all Michael cared. It had the desired effect. Butterflies were racing around in his stomach and he tried to sober up.

The accomplice was tall and gave the strong impression of a man looked like the type who was just waiting for the command to kill. He lurked behind Pickersgill, poised to act if necessary and then went and stood by Ingrid while Pickersgill was frisking Michael for possible weapons.

Ingrid opened the car door and Pickersgill told Michael to get in the back seat. He followed him in, holding the gun close to his ribs. The other man sat in the passenger seat next to Ingrid.

'Now drive,' said Pickersgill. '…follow instructions.'

Ingrid started the engine, moving off in the direction indicated by the accomplice.

Pickersgill was in an unfriendly, sarcastic mood.

'You just couldn't stay away, could you?' Pickersgill's sarcasm was plain. 'You had to be curious and return to the scene. Well Mr. Nosey Parker, what's your name again?'

'Michael - Michael Wright.'

'Well, Mr. Wright, you've got it all wrong. This is Berlin, not Brixton, and you're out of your depth. We've been watching the Mercedes from the derelict house opposite the carpark. You and that little lady, cruising around in her green Volkswagen, weren't hard to trace. You get around fast with the ladies, don't you? How's Cynthia?'

A chill went down Michael's spine. Now he knew for certain that he had done the right thing telling her to move in with Hyacinth. Pickersgill was trying to upset him mentioning Cynthia, perhaps believing that Ingrid knew nothing about her.

He tried to remain calm. He just couldn't figure out why he was again being held at gunpoint. The only thing he could think of was that he was now in real danger because of what he knew about Danny, Frank, and Mr Anastasia. Visiting the Mercedes had been a serious mistake.

'Do you know,' said Pickersgill, '…a true patriot of the Fatherland would have you shot for sleeping with a German woman. And you, little lady, are a disgrace to the German race and would be shot as well. But you're both lucky today. All I'm interested in is the contents of the Mercedes. No time for politics. And you can keep the car. See how generous I am.'

'Why don't you go and get it yourself?' said Michael, summoning the courage to sound arrogantly fearless. He wasn't just going to take Pickersgill's abuse as if he was some kind of lame duck. Any woman looking to a man for protection would expect some kind of reaction, physical or even verbal but it was hard to be a hero with a loaded gun in the ribs in the company of two psychopaths.

He paid the price for being so foolhardy. Pickersgill turned and slapped him across the side of the head with the revolver. The blow sent a zinging sound and a rush of pain to his brain. Stars appeared in front of his eyes.

'Shut up,' shouted Pickersgill. 'Getting the contents of that car for me is your only bargaining power for your lives. And I am a man of my word.'

It would be different if Pickersgill had been alone because he was sure he could overpower him but he imagined what a loaded gun fired at close range would do to him and he said nothing more.

Finally they reached a large house and Ingrid was told to park outside, blow the horn once and then flash her headlights twice. When she did so two more men emerged and Pickersgill wound the window down. 'We've got him,' he said.

Ingrid was then told to drive on to her flat. They arrived home in the small hours and prepared themselves mentally to spend a day of fear and uncertainty. Pickersgill searched the flat for weapons and told Ingrid not to answer the telephone which worried Michael because he knew that Cynthia would be telephoning sometime during the day. The last thing he wanted was for her to know anything was wrong let alone that they were being held at gunpoint.

While Pickersgill was searching the flat the thought crossed Michael's mind that Pickersgill would probably kill them after he got his gold. He couldn't bear thinking about it. Dying in Berlin would probably be a heroic, romantic story people who knew him were likely to tell long after he was gone but he didn't want to die in Berlin, or anywhere else, for any reason. And that was why he had no intention of making a grab for Pickersgill's gun until he was one hundred per cent sure he would succeed.

At some point Pickersgill called his accomplice by name for the first time so now Michael knew he was Wolfgang. Michael could see the animal resemblance in his eyes and his snarling, sinister grin. So far Wolfgang hadn't produced a gun but there was a bulge in his jacket to suggest he also had such a weapon. Whether he had or not the man was tall and built like a brick wall; he looked like someone who could endure any amount of punishment.

Since their ordeal had begun, Ingrid had remained silent, though sometimes looking at Michael through a slow trickle of tears. They weren't allowed to talk to each other and Michael couldn't think of a way to resolve the situation without doing what Pickersgill wanted. They both eventually fell asleep on the settee.

The continuous ringing of the telephone startled Michael awake and he opened his eyes. Feeling dizzy, and with a terrible headache, he felt the lump where his head had collided with Pickersgill's gun. Wolfgang was sitting opposite him and now he had a gun in his hand.

Ingrid opened her eyes too and looked around the room, as if uncertain what these strangers were doing in her flat.

The telephone kept ringing.

Pickersgill came out of the bedroom, his suit crumpled and his face gaunt. He had obviously slept with his clothes on and no longer looked much like didn't the distinguished supposedly English gentleman Michael had driven to Berlin. 'Don't touch it,' he shouted.

The telephone rang three more times and was silent.

Pickersgill pointed to Ingrid. 'You, go and make some coffee. Wolfgang, keep an eye on her just in case she has some poison she wants to get rid of in a hurry.'

'She won't do anything, boss. I'll make sure,' The reply came in English but with a coarse German accent. The accomplice seemed like nothing so much as an obediently crazy psychopath with the mind of a twelve year old shadowing Ingrid to the kitchen.

Pickersgill settled into an armchair and waving his gun casually in Michael's direction, said, 'Now listen carefully. That Mercedes in the car park has something in it that belongs to me and I'm going to get it. Let me re phrase that. You are going to get it for me. Understand?'

'You mean the gold?

'You're smart - much smarter than Danny. Mr Anastasia and Danny are bad businessmen. They stole a fortune from me because I trusted them while I was in hiding. That is why your friend Danny is in jail now and with one associate less than before. I've got connections everywhere. When you've got money you can buy any kind of service you want. So...'

Michael stared at him with contempt. He wanted to take the gun away and give him a few slaps, treating him as the arrogant schoolboy bully he appeared to be fully deserved.

'Now that you understand what's going on, I hope you'll toe the line and don't give me the opportunity to separate you from your breath.'

Michael nodded his acknowledgement without taking his eyes off Pickersgill. Then he said, 'What's in it for me?'

'Listen Mr. Not-So-Right, you're in no position to bargain. Your race had all the diamonds and gold in Africa and you let us take it from you. And what were your people doing? Singing songs about going to heaven and dancing. You'll certainly visit a heavenly world if you don't do as I say. But I've always been a reasonable and generous man, and if everything goes well, who knows.' He chuckled. 'After all, you brought me safely to Berlin and you deserve some credit for that. Besides, I find you interesting. I might even give you a – how would you say - wedge of money.'

'Is that before or after you shoot me?'

'Don't be pessimistic. Remember that fortune favours the brave. I'm a little disappointed in you though. Danny told me you are a law graduate. Well, that's what an English, bread-winning education system can do to you. It restricts one's thinking. In the process, it destroys your natural survival instinct. Mine is still intact. So tell me Mr. Wright, what happened to your African culture, your survival instincts? No, I'll tell you! The colonial system beat it out of you and replaced it with something they themselves don't believe in - religion. You became dependent on the white man and trusted him too much, because he gave you a God he imagined, an invisible man living in the sky. Your forefathers fell for it and took it all in. You have only yourselves to blame.'

Michael was becoming angry because he knew that some of what Pickersgill was saying almost made sense except that his ancestors had survived in spite of all the atrocities they had had to endure.

Just then Wolfgang and Ingrid came back with coffee and toast. There were tears in Ingrid's eyes. Michael felt guilty for getting her into the mess they were in.

Watching Pickersgill and Wolfgang as they ate and drank their coffees in silence Michael was trying to work out an escape plan, but couldn't think of anything. Before they finished their food, Michael broke the silence. 'The way I see it, Mr. Pickersgill, if I don't get the car for you, you can't get it, right? I know you're wanted. I telephoned England.'

'So did I, Mr. Wright, so did I. So we both know the score. And you know too much. I have friends everywhere who can take care of people who have too much information about me. We Germans fought the whole world by ourselves, so I'm not worried about other people. Just remember that.'

Michael wondered whether he had signed his own death warrant in revealing he already knew that what was hidden in the Mercedes was gold and that Pickersgill was a wanted criminal.

'We're all going for a driver later tonight and don't think of attracting the police, little lady. If you do, this gun will go off in Michael's face and Wolfgang will take care of you. We'll all then go to heaven together. But I know you don't want to die, pretty lady and neither does your lover. You've got so much to live for, Mr Wright, with two women in your life. Aren't you lucky?'

Ingrid could think of nothing to say in reply. She fixed her eyes on Pickersgill and waited as calmly as she could.

Pickersgill put a piece of paper with an address on the coffee table in the middle of the lounge. 'Tonight, Mr Wright, you're going to be a hero. I want you to take the Mercedes to this address. Ingrid can memorise it. She lives in Berlin so she should know where it is. A taxi will take you to the car park. And don't try anything smart. The driver is our man. When you get out of the taxi, walk slowly towards the car with Ingrid by your side, open the door for her, like a good chauffeur would, and drive. You know where the key is. That's all you've got to do. As soon as you deliver the car you're free to go.'

'That's exactly what you told me a few days ago when I drove you here.'

'That's true, but things have changed. In case fate tempts you and you try to make a run for it, Wolfgang is a fine marksman. He'll be opposite the car park with a rifle. From there he won't miss. By the way, everybody around me carries a gun, except you of course. And in case you hadn't realise it the reason you're doing the job is that if anyone gets caught it will be you.'

He said something to Wolfgang in what sounded Polish or Russian; then went to the telephone and made a call.

Going outdoors was the opportunity Michael was waiting for. It was the chance to work something out rather than trying to tackle Pickersgill and Wolfgang in a confined space. One possibility was that a police or soldier might stop them for a spot check and it would be better to be arrested than shot. If there was surveillance on the Mercedes and British and Americans were looking for a war criminal, they would probably shoot to kill and the authorities wouldn't care whether they captured Pickersgill and Wolfgang, dead or alive, or whether or not Michael was an accomplice or an innocent third party. He tried to think of a plan quickly before time ran out. All kinds of possibilities crossed his mind, some which didn't make sense. He had no real idea how to escape and was just hoping an ideal opportunity would present itself. As they sat in the living room passing time, he was becoming more nervous by the minute. The day had been long and drawn out, and neither he nor Ingrid had been allowed to leave the room to go further than the bathroom and only then with Wolfgang in tow.

Pickersgill made Ingrid press his crumpled trousers while he stayed in the bedroom. Wolfgang remained vigilant, menacing. As evening came and darkness fell, the tension in the room became almost unbearable. Pickersgill was pacing the floor and even Wolfgang seemed agitated. Ingrid became more nervous than ever as Pickersgill waved the gun about at the slightest sound or movement they made. Most intimidating of all was the silencer and knowing that death could come at a moment's notice without anyone hearing the shot.

It was about nine pm when the phone rang. The first thing that came to Michael's mind was that it was Cynthia. He came to the conclusion that Pickersgill would definitely tell her the situation he was in, a problem he didn't want her to know about. His heart pounded as Pickersgill reached for the receiver and answered in what sounded Russian or Polish. Michael gave a quiet, covert sigh of relief.

Another hour passed and Ingrid was becoming angry and frustrated at being made a prisoner in her own home. 'I've had enough of this. Bloody murderers, I've had enough,' she suddenly yelled.

'Shut up, before I lose my temper,' shouted back Pickersgill.

Michael grabbed her by the shoulders, trying to console her and whispering in her ear. 'If we want to live through this we have to do what he wants.' With Michael holding her, she calmed down.

It was another half an hour before the phone rang again and Pickersgill picked it up. He listened and then said: 'Let's go.'

They all got into Ingrid's car but before she could put the key in the ignition, Pickersgill said, 'One more thing before we leave. Wolfgang and me, we served in the same regiment during the war and we've killed before. So you better take us very seriously indeed. Now you can go.'

They drove around the city for about fifteen minutes, parked by a row of houses in the back streets near Charlottenburg, and waited for Pickersgill's next instructions. He pursed his lips and said, 'A taxi will take you to the car park from here. When you pick up the car, follow the taxi away, not too close and don't pass him. Another taxi will be following you.' Pickersgill had obviously planned for everything, including his own escape if necessary. It was no wonder he had managed to avoid capture for more than twenty years, and even travelled to and survived in England. By contrast Michael was depending on luck and opportunity. 'You'll get instructions as we go along. When you deliver the merchandise, you can go.'

'You expect us to believe you'll let us go free? People like you always make sure there are no witnesses to tell the tale.'

'Very clever, Mr. Wright, you've got a point. But I'm a gentleman, remember? And we Germans keep our word.'

'That sounds like the sort of fairy story they told to my ancestors when they were lured onto ships anchored off the West coast of Africa.'

'That probably was true in the past, Mr. Wright, but we Germans are more civilized and trustworthy. We have moral fibre, something many other Europeans are short of. I am sincere about my promises.'

'Your sincerity is as far back as your first piss, and that's a long, long, time ago.'

Mildly agitated, Michael waited for a response but none came. He knew he that even if he could take Pickersgill in a fight, and he probably could, he wasn't sure about Wolfgang whose height and massive frame oozed brute strength. Michel didn't think his boxing skills would be enough. He was outweighed by forty or fifty pounds and was at least two inches shorter.

Two taxis pulled up, one in front of Ingrid's car, the other behind it. There were two passengers in the back seat of the first taxi. The other taxi only contained a driver.

Pickersgill ordered Michael and Ingrid out of the Volkswagen and into the first taxi. Ingrid went in the front passenger seat and Michael sat between the two men in the back seat. It was a tight squeeze because one of the men was as big as Wolfgang. The other was tall and slim. To Michael he looked a cold-blooded knife killer. Perhaps even Transylvanian. The bigger man had his hand in his breast pocket, obviously carrying a gun. They both looked straight ahead, without making eye contact.

A third taxi turned up and Pickersgill and Wolfgang got into it and drove away immediately.

The snow was melting. The tyres of the taxis ploughed through the slush that now covered most of the city. Michael came to the conclusion that it would be fatal to try anything with three men in the car.

They travelled in silence, the driver occasionally glancing in his rear view mirror as if checking on Michael. Undisturbed snow on the pavement looked bright under the city's lights, almost pure, virginal. Michael was wondering if the city had a soul, a mind of its own, a consciousness, whether it would know that within its boundaries, lives were hanging on thin threads. Perhaps it could bring down divine intervention that would come to the aid of the helpless but he knew that was just wishful thinking in a time of crisis and desperation.

The lights ahead reflected on the windscreen and conjured weird images in his mind. Everything seemed so peaceful - the city, with its reflecting hue, from the snow, felt a place good people might go to when they die. Even though he trusted his imagination he knew that kind of perception was far removed from reality. It was a mere notion formed from baseless hope.

The taxi parked in a back street near to where the Mercedes was parked and the driver switched off his lights. The other taxi parked a little distance behind. Michael and Ingrid got out and walked towards the car park, passing the derelict house where Pickersgill had warned that Wolfgang would be waiting. The situation was tense but for the first time since their ordeal began, they had an opportunity to talk and try to work out an escape plan. However there was only one way in and out of the car park.

It wasn't an ideal place from which to start an escape. They agreed on that at least. Ingrid suggested they should make a run for it towards the military barracks, as soon as they got into the Mercedes and reached the main road. The barracks were about four miles away. Michael reminded her that all the men were armed and that would be too risky.

They reached the Mercedes and he opened the door to let Ingrid in as Pickersgill had instructed. Next he cleared the snow from the roof, bonnet and windscreen and then got into the driver's seat. The keys were in the glove compartment where he had left them.

'What are we going to do, Michael?'

'I don't know yet. Let's get the car started.'

He put the key in the ignition and the engine fired at the third attempt. He revved it a few times, turned the car around and slowly headed for the exit. The taxi drivers switched their headlights on and started their engines as he pulled out onto the main road. One taxi came round in front of the Mercedes and the other taxi fell in behind. Michael could only wish for some military or local police to come upon them and to arrest him and everybody else. It was after all almost midnight and they were passing Spandau Prison and the nearby British military barracks but, as usual, there was never a policeman or soldier in sight when one was most needed. There seemed no plausible means to get away.

'That address we're going to…we have to pass through the city centre to reach it. There'll be people around even though the weather is bad. We can't just leave everything to chance. We've got to try and plan what to do before we reach the city centre.'

'I hear you, Ingrid. I'm trying to think.'

'What if we deliberately have an accident in the city centre?'

'I don't want to get shot, but I don't want to die in a car accident either. We can't afford to take any chances unless we're sure we can get away.'

'Well I don't care anymore. We're going to die anyway if we don't do something fast.'

'Just shut up, Ingrid, shut up.'

She was becoming hysterical and he was losing his composure but he knew she was right. They had to do something and quickly. He just couldn't think what.

As they approached a set of traffic lights, a car overtook them and tucked in behind the taxi they were following. They looked at each other. The traffic lights stayed on red for what seemed an unusually long time. That bought some more thinking time. He decided that if the taxi in front indicated left or right, or began to turn, he would go in the opposite direction and try to make a getaway. But the car that had overtaken them was too close to allow them to see in which direction the taxi in front was going and the taxi behind was so close, it was almost touching the Mercedes' bumper.

The lights turned green, the car in front began to turn left and then they could see the taxi turning right. Michael could see the driver checking his mirror to make sure they were following. He would have slammed the Mercedes into a left-hand turn but the other car was driving too slowly and there wasn't enough room to pass him and make a getaway in the snow.

He saw it as a missed opportunity.

They reached a signpost half covered in mud and snow and he recognised the area. Ingrid had driven past there a few days earlier. While he drove he looked around to get his bearings. The streets were narrow and the traffic slow moving. He knew they were running out of time and he needed to do something. 'How far is it from here?'

'About five miles. By the edge of the Grunewald forest. If we get there, they'll never let us go. People have been killed there before now.'

He recognised the fear in her voice and that made him more nervous. 'Why didn't you tell me that?'

'I was too frightened to remember. If we go there no one will be able to help us.'

'Then we're not leaving the city. If we're going to die, let's die where everyone can see us and hope that Pickersgill and his friends are caught.'

The traffic lights up ahead turned red. Michael gripped the steering wheel tightly as the lights turned green, told Ingrid to hold on and swung the car sharply left into a one-way street. The Mercedes skidded and climbed the pavement, just missing oncoming traffic. The taxi behind tried to follow but ran straight into oncoming traffic and came to a standstill.

Michael accelerated the Mercedes, bobbing and weaving through traffic. The car belched clouds of black smoke as the wheels fought for traction in the snow. It climbed the pavement again, swerving, narrowly missing cars as they tried to get out of the way. He looked in his rear view mirror. The taxi that had been in front when they started out was now in pursuit and another unmarked car had joined the chase. Soon they were back in traffic and heading for the heart of the city. He didn't care which direction he was going in. He just wanted to put distance between himself and his pursuers. The fact that he was driving a car loaded with gold bullion was far from his mind. His only interest was in survival, in escape and evasion.

He reached another traffic light, just turning red and sped through. As he turned left three unsilenced shots rang out and Ingrid screamed and crouched down on the floor. A fourth shot came right through the rear windscreen. They made a right turn and a police car going the opposite direction spun around in their wake to follow them. A military police jeep came out of another side road and it too joined the chase. A burst of automatic fire shattered both the rear window and the front windscreen of the Mercedes. Ingrid screamed as the car careered onto the pavement, skidded again, hit a lamp post and came to a violent stop its radiator gushing water and steam.

There were more shots, but this time, to Michael, they seemed distant. There was darkness as he slid into unconsciousness.

CHAPTER FOURTEEN

Darkness slowly turned to light as Michael opened his eyes to the noise of a door being slammed and the sound of heavy boots. They interrupted a hazy sleep that bordered on unconsciousness. He found himself in a strange environment, on his back, in a small bed. He stared at the ceiling as he opened his eyes. Nothing seemed to make sense. His chest and head ached and he could feel dried blood on the side of his face.

A tall soldier in British uniform came into focus. Another soldier was behind him, rifle at the ready. The nearest soldier shouted: 'He's coming round, sir.'

The shout prompted the arrival of a man in civilian clothes and wearing a shoulder holster, with the butt of a revolver clearly visible as he approached, Michael tried to figure out where he was and what was happening, but he couldn't remember anything. What he did know for sure was he wasn't in a house or hospital.

'Where am I?'

'Spandau Prison and you're under arrest,' said the man in the civilian suit. He was calm and well spoken. Michael guessed he was either an officer or a member of the British Secret Service. He came closer and stood over Michael. 'Don't you remember anything?' He paused and waited for an answer. When none came, he said, 'You were in a car crash.'

Michael looked around and tried to clear his head as the man waited patiently for an answer. Finally he said, 'Well son, you better think fast because you're in a lot of trouble. You've got some explaining to do.' He paused giving Michael time to think.

The name Spandau jogged Michael's memory, but the

overwhelming headache and pains all over his body threatened imminent unconsciousness again. He summoned the determination to stay awake. 'Isn't this where Hess and Speer are locked up?' he asked, narrowing his eyes to get some relief from his excruciating headache. He meant that Rudolf Hess, Hitler's Deputy, and Albert Speer the Nazi architect. He had read long ago about Hess's capture while trying to surrender in Scotland but could never have imagined a few months ago, that he'd be end up in the same place to be interrogated.

'Hess is...not too far from here and we've got enough room for more spies.'

'I'm not a spy, I'm just a chauffeur.'

'You'll have a job convincing anyone about that. You've got yourself mixed up with a bunch of undesirables wanted by both British and American intelligence. Your Mr. Pickersgill, real name Hans Weiderfelt, and his side-kick Wolfgang Hampel, are wanted for war crimes and espionage. You're smack in the middle of it all.' He pulled up a chair closer to the bed and sat down. 'You were driving a stolen car, owned by a VIP and had nearly £500 in your pocket.'

Michael felt a sour taste in his mouth. It was a taste, generated by fear. The penalty for spying in wartime was death, or, at the very least, long-term imprisonment. That's what Garry Powers had faced when he was shot down over Russia in his U-2 spy plane and for Michael it was clear that he was facing the same threatened future.

He tried to sit up in bed, assisted by one of the solders on the instructions of the interrogator. As he looked at the man, he came to the conclusion that he was an agent, rather than regular army. Alarm bells were ringing in his head again alongside real fear and anxiety over the predicament he was now in. To be locked up in

Spandau next to war criminals was more than just a bridge too far. He wasn't sure how he was going to talk his way out of this, or whether his law degree would help him but it was obviously in his best interest to tell the interrogator whatever he wanted to know…if he knew the answers in the first place. From what he had heard Spandau Prison was a frighteningly lonely place to spend even one night.

'You remember the name Pickersgill, don't you?'

As soon as the name was mentioned, things locked away in the back of his mind slowly began to surface. He could vaguely remember the car chase and recalled shots being fired before the crash. Then he remembered that Ingrid was in the car with him during the chase.

'Yes,' He wipe a trace of blood from his lips with the back of his hand. 'Where's Ingrid? Can I see a doctor?'

'All in good time. Ingrid is in hospital with cuts and bruises; but she'll live. Wolfgang is quite dead, I can assure you, and our friend alias Pickersgill is somewhere in the city. But we'll soon get him. And by the way, you are here to answer questions, not to ask them.' He then called out to the duty sergeant to telephone the doctor.

'Someone from the medical staff will be along here soon. Now what's your story - the whole story? Take your time, there's no hurry. You're not going anywhere, and I have lots of time.' He sat down on the chair again with a note pad in his hand awaiting Michael's response.

Michael didn't know where to begin. For the next fifteen minutes, he struggled to remember things in any detail. He tried to concentrate and focused on recalling events over the past months. He began by talking about the first time he met Danny at university and what happened from the first day he arrived in

Birmingham. He tried to put everything in chronological order, although that was difficult. He told his interrogator the story the best way he could but was astute enough not to disclose that he knew the cars he had sprayed were stolen, or how much money he had earned for spraying them. He was, however, prepared to give what information he possessed about Mr Anastasia and Danny. That was little enough and mainly gleaned from what Barbara had told him over the telephone.

He went on to outline his experiences since first meeting Pickersgill, until the moment the Mercedes crashed. Finally he told the interrogator about the gold welded into the secret compartments in the Mercedes. He didn't want to spend any time in Spandau Prison if he could help it and was no longer prepared to protect anyone else, least of all Danny. The only thing on his mind was his freedom, so he could go home to Cynthia.

The interrogator listened carefully, occasionally interrupting, asking for more details as he took notes. The session lasted for more than an hour by which time Michael was exhausted from fatigue, pain, and the sheer pressure of being questioned.

Just before the end a uniformed army doctor walked in with a stethoscope around his neck. He examined Michael, cleaned the blood from his bruised face and said he had no serious injuries. He gave him some painkillers and a warm drink before leaving.

The interrogator said he was going to check out Michael's story and left shortly after. As he was leaving Michael asked if he could see a lawyer. He got no reply.

Michael wasn't sure how much of what he had said would be believed. At one point, the interrogator had told him that parts of his story were flimsy but he had told the whole truth, as far as he could remember. He didn't want to become a permanent resident of Spandau and it seemed to him that withholding information now could only make his offences even more serious. The military, or the British government could after all make any decision they wanted, as to his fate and there was nothing anyone could do about it.

It crossed Michael's mind that he probably wouldn't see Cynthia, Ingrid, Uncle Ben, Sweet Man and all the other people that were closest to him, for a very long time. He didn't want news of his predicament to reach his mother, or anyone else really. She had paid for his education so he could become a good lawyer when he returned to Jamaica. Instead, he was now in a Berlin prison, locked up with notorious war criminals, and accused of spying. If word got out about his incarceration, he imagined the scandal, especially in Jamaica. Most people he had ever known believed you must be an ambassador for Jamaica when you got to travel abroad. He thought about some of the possible reactions from older people, rattled by the notion of a poor one-parent mother, struggling to educate a worthless son. 'Dat bwoy is worthless. Imagine his maddah gone to Canada to work and school de bwoy to be a lawyer. An what him go an do? De bwoy get himself mix up wid car thief, bullion robber and war criminals. Dat bwoy don't have no ambishan. Ah just feel sorry fe de poor maddah.'

By the time the story reached Jamaica and was retold time after time, there would be bound to be at least fifty different versions and his notoriety would be so widespread, it wouldn't be worth going back to Jamaica. The story would sure make the front page of the Jamaican paper, *The Daily Gleaner.* Ending up in Spandau prison was almost the ultimate disaster, just a marginally better option than the one Pickersgill probably had had in store for him. At least he was alive even though...not so well.

For now at least he felt reasonably physically safe. With Wolfgang dead, Pickersgill and his band of little Caesars would be completely pre-occupied in trying to avoid capture. He began to be a touch more optimistic that everything would be all right when they discovered he was telling the truth. But that didn't suppress all his anxieties.

Several hours after the interrogator left, he was helped to another cell. By this time he could barely walk. The effects of the car crash had over powered the pain killers. The door was slammed and bolted and he was instantly overwhelmed by claustrophobia from childhood memories.

He looked around the small cell, trying to familiarise himself with his new surroundings and then hobbled towards the small bed and fell on top of it. Now depressed and totally sorry for himself, he realised that he had never ever been locked up in a room before. It felt traumatic. It certainly didn't feel like part of the adventure which he started with Danny several months ago. This wasn't a game anymore, but a surreal and nasty experience. And as the interrogator had earlier reassured him, he wasn't going anywhere.

The cell door opened after a few hours, just as he was about to fall asleep. Two soldiers came in. One carried food on a tray; the other held a rifle absurdly at the ready. Even if they had swung the cell door and front gate open and told him to leave, he wouldn't have had the strength to walk away. The soldier put the tray of food on the floor without saying a word and left.

He tried the food but could barely chew or swallow. Eating became an exercise in pain management.

With nothing to do or no one to talk to, passing the time was tedious. He had nothing to occupy himself with except reflecting on the events of the last weeks and months. He tried to shut them out and failed. Instead they replayed in his mind over and over again.

At one point, he tried to blame some childhood, traumatic experience, for driving him to behave irrationally but that idea was quickly dismissed. Eventually he told himself the truth. Desire for money and stupidity were responsible for his predicament.

In his private and isolated domain, he listened to soldiers' conversations from out in the corridor. They ranged from the sublime to the outrageous and included any number of racist jokes. It was entertainment of a kind. Seeing as there was nothing else on offer, he took it all in.

Some soldiers were even giving away information about military operations, without realising what they were saying. Others talked passionately about their personal lives and the loved ones they were missing and how it affected them. A few sounded as if they needed urgent counselling.

From what Michael overheard, he began to realise that everyone had some kind of story to tell. It was a world, filled with conflicting and contrasting experiences.

Throughout the long night, listening to the changing of the guards, in between being half asleep and half awake, he took in more of those casual revelations. Some were unhappy that they never get real recognition for the job they do for their country. Others didn't seem to know much about why they even were in Berlin, apart from the job of guarding Spandau Prison. One soldier expressed fears that, if a war started, Berlin would be the first target for a nuclear bomb. Their prevailing philosophy seemed to be to kill, or prepare to die whichever was demanded of them. They all seemed to believe that their government was right and everybody else was wrong. He guessed some of their sentiments were born not out patriotism, but of military indoctrination and conditioning.

He got out of bed and looked through the small window that overlooked part of the prison grounds. There was barbed wire and an electric fence in addition to the high prison wall and sentry boxes. Intermittently search lights scanned the prison walls and grounds. He watched the searchlights shining on the skyline. Eventually, he climbed back into bed, worn out, and without even the desire or energy to wrestle with his thoughts any more.

The following day was uneventful; boring. With nothing to do, it was hardly worth getting off his bed for. He went to sleep very early in the evening.

A scream startled him awake. He opened his eyes and sat up in bed. His watch told him it was five minutes to midnight. At first he thought he'd been dreaming. He waited in silence and listened.

It came again; this time much louder. Then everything was quiet again.

Whoever was screaming, and for whatever reason, had no chance of being heard outside the prison walls. No one would or could come to their aid. Spandau was fortress, with several reinforcing army barracks close by containing hundreds of soldiers.

Perhaps someone was having nightmares, or had lost their mind. The other possibility that crossed Michael's mind was that maybe someone was being tortured but he couldn't think of any reason why long term prisoners like Rudolf Hess would be being tortured after all these years. Unless there was information someone still wanted, about other war criminals. In Berlin, anything was possible but he dismissed that idea.

The screams continued at intervals for about an hour and he became more restless. When he couldn't take it anymore he started knocking on the door of his prison cell.

After about five minutes he heard footsteps approaching. The small peep-hole in the cell door was slid open and a loud, grumpy voice shouted, 'What do you want, Sambo?'

'What's that noise?'

'Don't worry about it, Sam. You'll get used to it. It's just Herr Hess getting one of his turns. Mad as a hatter. 'Hasn't had a woman for more than twenty years.'

There was laughter from another soldier. 'If you were locked up all those years without a woman, you'd be crying as well. Isn't that right corporal?'

'That's right sergeant, that's what happens to anyone who gets locked up in Spandau. No freedom and no sex.'

'And how much time do you think they'll give this boy, corporal?'

'Life, sergeant, at least. Maybe they'll put him in the same cell as Hess and they can have fun together.'

'I don't think so, corporal. I'm sure Hess won't like Sambo. Don't forget he's a Nazi and you know what Nazis think of coloured people. They're not blonde or pure Arian race. Now go to sleep, Sam, and shut your fucking mouth. Get back into bed and no wanking on government property.'

Just then, someone shouted that the duty officer was on his way. The peep-hole was slammed shut and soon everything was back to normal, as if nothing at all unusual had happened.

It was a moment of reckoning, a realisation of how helplessness and isolation can make you surrender to your fate. It was a feeling he didn't want to get used to or experience for long. He was now losing all desire to sleep and even wished he could see the interrogator again. At least he had been polite and seemed to have some decision-making powers. Maybe he was the one who would decide Michael's fate. He looked out of the small window again, following the searchlight as it lit the surrounding areas. The moment felt unreal, as if he was observing the whole experience

151

from a distance but he knew that was like wishing to go to the moon on a bicycle.

He got back into bed and was even more restless as he listened to the intermittent screams which continued until almost daybreak.

The sound of a distant bugle playing *Reveille* caused him to open his eyes. Not too long after, someone began banging his cell door. He looked at his watch. It was 6.15.

He could hear soldiers marching to commands. The cell door opened; and food was passed to him on a tray, observed by another soldier with rifle at the ready. Breakfast was a repeat of the menu from previous days. It wasn't the kind of ritual to stimulate appetite but he was aware of the fact that he wasn't in a restaurant in Soho and complaining about the service would have been an exercise in stupidity. He did what anyone in his position would do. He ate what was given to him, without complaining, then lay on his bed and hoped for the best.

About midday, he heard the changing of the guards and got up to look out of his cell window. The snow had melted and the sun was out. It was then that he saw a lone figure, more than six feet tall, hands behind his back, walking in the prison grounds and realised that it must be Hess on his daily walk. He was tramping around in circles, like a trapped animal with nowhere to go. He watched him for about half an hour, thinking about the circumstances that must have brought him to his present predicament. For all he knew Rudolf Hess might have been a political victim who wanted peace, rather than a war criminal, or a representative of Hitler. From what he had read years earlier there was no real evidence that Hess had committed atrocities on the scale of Hermann Goring, the Luftwaffe chief, or Heinrich Himmler, head of the feared SS. Those two men had borne so much of the responsibility for wartime atrocities. But then just to be Hitler's deputy must have been a serious crime, considering what Hitler did to the Jews and everyone else but instead of hanging Hess they gave him life imprisonment

Michael thought a lot about the events of World War Two none of which had anything to do with his present predicament.

Weeks passed with the same prison routines. He was given fresh clothes and even managed to have a conversation with a sympathetic, Scottish Duty Sergeant, who listened to what he had to say, sympathetically. But he was powerless to do anything. He told Michael that as far as he knew, no official charges had been brought against him and that their orders were that he was not to be abused verbally or physically. That made him feel more secure, knowing that there was some kind of rule of law that offered him some protection. He managed over time to adjusted to being in a confined space but was still tormented by the occasional screams of Rudolf Hess at night.

Then the screaming became less frequent. *Perhaps they had sedated or somehow silenced him*, he thought.

With so much time on his hands, he tried to work out what the relationships must be between Danny, Mr Anastasia, and Pickersgill. Danny's accountancy skills would have been deployed to cover up the underworld activities for them all. He knew that Danny was audacious and would know how to launder money, evade taxes, and make their business operations look legitimate. As a reward for his work, he must have had a large share of the cake, probably including the proceeds of past war crimes as well as more recent dodgy business operations. He couldn't help reflecting on the surprise party Danny took him to the first weekend he arrived in Birmingham. He remembered the lavish lifestyles they were all enjoying and the extent to which Mr. Anastasia had seemed to be revered by everyone around him.

But none of that mattered now.

CHAPTER FIFEEN

More than a month passed in isolation, loneliness and uncertainty. He was living in a world that did not exist outside his prison walls.

After one restless night, he was up earlier than usual. He could hear soldiers going through their routine but shortly after, to his considerable surprise, his cell door was flung opened and the interrogator walked in.

'Get dressed.'

He didn't even wait for a reaction. He turned and walked away and a soldier slammed the door shut again. A few minutes later the cell door was opened again and the travelling case Michael had left at Ingrid's place was thrown into the cell. He didn't know the reason or what was going to happen, but felt a sudden optimism. He hoped whatever else was coming that he would be taken outdoors - a welcome respite from confinement. Several more weeks of isolation would probably have pushed him over the edge and he desperately wanted to be a part of the outside world again - to see daylight from the outside.

He got dressed as fast as he could, sat on his bed and waited.

The interrogator returned about half an hour later. He was smartly dressed and carrying a travel bag. He took a pair of handcuffs from his back pocket, clipped one half to Michael's wrist and the other to his own and tilted his head to one side, indicating that it was time to go.

Two soldiers escorted them as they headed towards the army Land Rover parked by prison gate. Behind them the cell door slammed shut and for the first time in more than six weeks, Michael felt a glimmering sense of freedom. It was the freedom to breathe air not encased in concrete, freedom to look forward to being in the company of other people. For the moment he didn't care much where they were taking him. He just wanted to be as far away as possible from Spandau.

They drove through some familiar streets, not least one of the streets along which he had been pursued driving the Mercedes in his attempt to escape from Pickersgill. They travelled in silence, at high speed, as if they were late for an appointment.

A sign up ahead said *Tempel Hof Airport*. In the distance planes could be seen taking off and landing.

Within fifteen minutes of his arrival at the airport, he was on board a Dutch KLM aircraft, with England his stated destination. His handcuff was removed and he was free to fasten his seatbelt and prepared for take-off.

From the time they had left Spandau Prison there had been no conversation between himself and the interrogator. As soon as they were airborne Michael ended that state of affairs. 'I know I'm not supposed to ask question.'

'No you're not.'

'Can I just ask you one question? Where are we going?'

'England, old chap. You're getting a free passage back to Blighty to stand trial. You'll have access to a lawyer as soon as you get there.'

'What happened to Ingrid?'

'She was in custody, but is out on bail. There's still the question of her relationship with you and all the other villains. And we're still checking out her story. Now no more questions.'

Michael turned his head and looked out of the window at the

landscape below, happy to be putting distance between himself and Spandau. That emotion, however, didn't completely overcome his fear of flying. As the plane climbed above clouds, and turbulence, he became uneasy again. This was only his second ever flight after all. And in his mind's eye, he still could picture the ugly sight of the prison and was tormented by questions. He kept asking himself if he had been the victim of circumstances or a callous, miscalculating fool? That would all have to be left to a jury. At least he was on his way back to England and that offered a lot of comfort.

The plane landed at Gatwick in scudding wind and driving rain. He was handcuffed and quickly ushered through customs. With an unlooked for sense of humanity the interrogator did his best to cover up the handcuffs as other passengers looked on. They climbed into another waiting Land Rover and it took them to Colchester Barracks where he was quickly locked away in a cell with brisk army efficiency. He had heard that Colchester was a correction centre for soldiers who had fallen foul of military law and had a reputation for being draconian.

Before long he could hear the voice of a non-commissioned officer shouting commands. He wondered why they had taken him there. He was a civilian, not a soldier and couldn't understand it at all.

Colchester Barracks proved a radical change after Spandau. There wasn't the same sense of isolation or the disturbing screams at night, although he could hear soldiers being subjected to verbal abuse but he had already learned that shouting and verbal abuse were simply an integral part of army life.

A week passed, and again life became tedious. From his cell, he could hear a lot of activity, but the only people he saw were the soldiers who brought his meals and those checking his cell to make sure he was still there and the sense of isolation began to return.

He wasn't quite sure how much more he could take and was now desperate to see a familiar face again – even the interrogator. All he now wanted was a conclusion to the nightmare, whatever the final outcome. Being locked away for months without being charged or given access to a solicitor was painful enough. Having no contact with friends, family of loved ones was becoming harder and harder to bear, especially not knowing what was happening. And even trying to sleep peacefully for long hours was impossible because of barracks activity, as well as the recurring dreams and flashbacks.

It was late at night and he was trying to empty all thoughts from his mind and prepare himself mentally to get some sleep. The key went into the lock of his cell door and a soldier with a rifle walked in and to his fierce joy the man was accompanied by the interrogator.

He was told to get dressed. Without hesitation, he quickly packed his bag and was handcuffed and taken briskly to yet another waiting Land Rover. It all happened with a cloak and dagger efficiency reminiscent of some undercover operation. But going outdoors had now become a hugely special treat for Michael.

Fifteen minutes into his journey it began to rain heavily. He nestled up to his travelling bag and tried to get a clearer view of where they were heading in the driving rain. It was hard to see anything in the darkness and he eventually fell asleep. When he opened his eyes, the rain had become drizzle and he could see a signpost ahead. They were heading into London. He felt a sense of elation, knowing that he was getting closer to people who cared about him, although they didn't know where he was. He thought about Cynthia, but disguised his anxiety, remaining calm and not asking questions. The only reason he could imagine for them bringing him back from Germany was that they believed his story and he was going to be tried in England. As far as he was concerned, he had done nothing wrong except being stupid enough to get involved with Danny and his associates. He thought they had probably discovered that the accusation of spying and collaborating with the enemy were nonsense. Someone had obviously checked his background to verify things he had told the interrogator although he knew he could still be found guilty by association.

The gates of Brixton Prison swung open in the small hours of the morning and he was briskly taken to a cell and locked away. Unable to sleep in another unfamiliar, strange environment, he spent most of the night thinking. In between worrying, the sounds made by other inmates gave him an odd sense of security. At least he wasn't isolated anymore and there would be some sort of legal process, later. He knew that would give him the chance to tell his side of the story, in court. But he wasn't complacent. He knew he had to prove his innocence and that wasn't going to be easy. He was aware of injustices meted out to people merely because of their skin colour, or due to lies told by prosecutors and the police, or simply because victims couldn't afford a good lawyer. He knew that some, so called Christians, sometimes even lied after swearing with their hand on the Bible - not very good Christians!

Sweet Man's teachings echoed through his mind. He had to learn quickly to adjust to civilian prison life, in a constructive, disciplined, way and he knew that to obey the strictures of the system was most likely the best option.

From the outset some inmates regarded him suspiciously, and a few prison officers behaved as if they had heard why he was there. One pugged-nosed, eccentric looking warden, who could have easily passed for a homicidal maniac, took an instant disliking to him. He didn't disguise his feelings and would prod him with his baton, at the least opportunity. He would complete the provocation with racist remarks. Michael could see in his eyes that he was waiting for him to react, as an excuse to use his baton so he did exactly as he was told and tried to keep on the good side of everyone.

Apart from meal times, he was kept locked in his cell all day. Throughout the week, he tried to remain nonchalant, not wanting to attract unnecessary attention. He formed a relationship with an inmate named Neville, another Jamaican. He was a deserter from the army, because of the racist treatment he received during his service. And had been dishonourably discharged. Then after committing several fairly minor offences, he ended up in Brixton Prison. He was in his late twenties and reminded Michael as a younger version of Uncle Ben. He seemed to have an excessive passion for women and nightlife. Through conversations during meal times, Michael discovered that Neville knew his way around London, and Brixton in particular, like the back of his hand. He mentioned some places that Michael knew although that wasn't too surprising. If you were black and living in London, Brixton was one of the places you would go for entertainment.

Neville told him that inmates had 'heard Michael was a spy in Berlin, which Neville had told them was bullshit. Most believed him. 'They know there's no black spies. Why should a white man use a black man as a spy, when they're spying on us as well? They wouldn't let us know any spy secrets, because they think we'd go and tell our brethren and mash up their runnings.'

That explanation brought a laugh from Michael, something he hadn't done for a long time. He wished Neville could be in court to repeat it. A judge might well agree. On the other hand, a different judge might interpret his comment as presumptuous; too smart for his own good.

He told Neville he was a chauffeur and was arrested after driving a man to Berlin. He didn't disclose anything else, or try to form a closer relationship. Sweet Man had told him that, in prison you meet all kinds of people who tell you different things, and sometimes very little of it was true. Giving too much information about yourself to inmates could be disastrous. Some inmates could crucify you by giving prison authorities, or inmates, a different story, to make sure you do real time. Besides, sometimes forming an alliance, or becoming part of a clan in a prison environment, is not a good idea even if it offered protection and support. The down side was that once integrated you became subject to their code of conduct, wrongly or rightly. With people wanting power and status in such a confined space from which there is no escape, there are always dangers.

Sweet Man's words kept ringing in his ears and Michael tried to put into practice what he'd been told. Sweet Man had spoken from first-hand experience. He had been wrongfully arrested once on his way home from a Saturday night party and charged with assaulting the police.

In any event Michael was hoping that his stay in Brixton would be short so he maintained friendship with Neville with a degree of caution.

A bunch of keys announced the arrival of a prison officer at his cell door. He opened his eyes as the key was inserted into the lock and the cell door flung open. The officer entered, baton drawn and looking prepared to use it. Following behind was the familiar figure of Michael's Spandau interrogator.

The prison officer accompanied them only as far as a small office and then it was just the two of them. It was the reunion he had been waiting for. Although they hardly had any proper conversation since that first interview, he knew the interrogator was his possible passport to freedom.

The man was in a more relaxed mood, a complete contrast to the other times they had met. He wasn't exactly overtly friendly, but he seemed much more at ease. It was as if he had come to the conclusion that Michael was just a misguided soul who had fallen into the wrong company. He sat behind the desk, told Michael to take a seat, opened his briefcase and took out a folder.

There was silence, except for the rustle of documents. The interrogator selected a few and laid them out on the desk. 'These are your statements and other papers about your case. Officially, you haven't been charged with anything yet. Let's say you were being held in custody while we continued our investigations. We've checked your story and fortunately for you, most of what you told us seems to be true. What still concerns us is your relationship with Danny Hogarth and if you were really colluding with him. That is for the police authorities to pursue.'

'But I don't know anything or anyone in Birmingham, apart from the names of the people I told you about.'

'That's still to be determined so you'll have to tell me again in as much detail as you can remember. You've had enough time for your memory to recover. You want to see Cynthia, don't you?'

'Or course. When can I see her?'

'All in good time. Now start talking; from the beginning.'

Michael did as he was told. He began by talking about his experience since he arrived in England and his student days, when he first met Danny. It was a nervous moment as he tried to recall as much as he could, in chronological order. He didn't want to contradict whatever was already in the interrogator's files. He told him everything he could remember, up to the moment the Mercedes crashed. The interview lasted over an hour. He even talked about his hopes and dreams, but later felt embarrassed that he had.

Throughout the interview, his interrogator was silent as he listened, and took notes. At the end he compared the fresh statements with those in the documents from his briefcase. When he was satisfied that he had all the information he needed, he put all his papers back into his brief case and leaned back in his chair. 'Wanting to be a solicitor and finding yourself in jail after university, isn't a good start to your career. A judge might not take too kindly to that sort of behaviour. You're supposed to be a man looking forward to practising law. You are bringing the legal profession into disrepute. For that you could get a custodial sentence.'

Michael remained silent, because he knew that statement was about right. He had no answer. He continued to sit in silence, child-like, acknowledging only by nodding. He felt he was being reprimanded but justifiably. By this time his head was hanging low, looking towards the floor and displaying remorse.

Into the pregnant silence, the interrogator dropped his news. 'You'll be pleased to hear that the charge of espionage has been dropped.'

Michael could hardly believe what he was hearing. He raised his head, with a surprised look on his face and thanked him.

'Don't thank me. If there were any evidence that you were collaborating with Pickersgill and his associates, you'd be spending a very long time in prison. Whether you do any real time of course will depend on your further cooperation in the future. We might need you as a witness to put away Mr Anastasia and some of his friends.'

Michael could only agree to co-operate to the fullest extent. He felt like throwing his arms around his interrogator, in total gratitude but didn't think that would have been appreciated. The prison officer outside might have rushed in thinking what he was witnessing was an assault. Michael thanked the interrogator again and promised he would tell him anything else he wanted to know in future.

'Don't thank me. Just doing my job. I couldn't imagine a Jamaican being a spy. My assumptions were right, fortunately for you.'

'Can you tell me anything about Ingrid? And when can I see Cynthia?'

'Ingrid was held by the German police, but has now been released without charge. We're working with the German police and they believed her story. If nothing else, it seems you were enjoying yourself with Ingrid in Berlin. I'm sure when your lady in London knows about that she won't be too pleased.'

It was a sore point to be reminded that there were two women in his life and one which brought back mixed emotions. He was in love with one and unsure of the true extent of his affection for the other. He tried to recapture images of the time he had spent with Ingrid but and his overwhelming desire to see Cynthia took over.

The sound of the interrogator's voice brought him back to reality; 'Pickersgill and some of his friends have been arrested. He said that the first time you both met was when you drove him to Berlin which fitted with your side of the story. Danny is still in jail awaiting trial on multiple charges and Barbara is back in Nigeria. We'll find her of course and the search is still on for Mr. Anastasia. We know he's got a yacht anchored near one of the Greek islands.'

'When am I going to see Cynthia?'

'I've arranged a visit. A solicitor and Cynthia. You'll see them both in a few days.'

Of course Michael needed a solicitor and wanted his freedom but seeing Cynthia was now more important to him. It made him angry with himself for causing so much mental pain to her and so many other people too. He just wanted to reassure himself that she was alright emotionally. That would soothe his own restlessness and banish most of his fears for the future.

Ingrid was in his mind for different reasons. Their brief encounter had developed into an emotional attachment too of sorts. Fate had led them into each other's path and she had taken good care of him in Berlin. He wanted to contact her to see how she was and to apologise for all the distress he had caused her. He wanted to keep in touch, even if only as a platonic friend.

'You're a very lucky man. Now that I'm recommending the charge of spying be dropped, you'll be given leniency for turning Queen's evidence. We want you to help us bring some people who think they're above the law, to justice. You'll be charged with spraying cars, in the knowledge that they were stolen. Of course you can deny that but I'm not going to put words in your mouth. I shouldn't be having this conversation with you and if you repeat it I shall deny we ever did.'

'What conversation?' was the response, as Michael tried to inject a sudden feeling of light heartedness in what was still a very serious situation.

'Never promise a policeman that you'll help him in future, because you'll eventually become an informer.'

That's just what Sweet Man had once said.

Michael couldn't help thinking about those words of advice. But in his situation, he had no choice. He had learned enough now the hard way about what to do and what wasn't a good idea when dealing with the law. Now, here he was, abandoning Sweet Man's wisdom, making promises to an interrogator, or a policeman - he still wasn't quite sure which. In the black community, he would forever after be known as a police informer for keeping such a promise but he didn't care about that. All he wanted was his freedom. For freedom, he, like most people, would promise anything. Anyway he planned to put some considerable distance between himself and Europe as soon as he was freed. He wanted to be five thousand miles away, in the Caribbean.

At the end, his interrogator thanked him for his cooperation and wished him luck. His final words were, 'I'll see you in court.'

Michael agreed that he would. Now that he was in Brixton prison and close to home, he wasn't going to do anything stupid that would jeopardise his freedom. Cynthia and the solicitor would be visiting him and hopefully he would be bailed soon.

He was taken back to his cell and spent the rest of the day contemplating his probable release from prison. He didn't tell anyone, including Neville, the news.

CHAPTER SIXTEEN

Cynthia, Hyacinth and Sweet Man came through the door with the rest of the visitors. There were mixed emotions as everyone tried to come to terms with the situation. Michael was happy to see Cynthia and they both shed tears, unashamedly. He couldn't explain his feelings, or even tried to. The joy of seeing her, and the familiar faces of Sweet Man and Hyacinth, brought out all the months of pent up emotion. There was a lot of things to talk about and he didn't know where to even begin.

It took a while before the overflowing emotions were put to rest. He tried to talk about some of his experiences over the past months, since he started working for Danny. Talking about those experiences was difficult but at least he could now talk freely if he could, without the feeling of being interrogated. It was also an opportunity to empty himself emotionally.

He tried to paint a clear picture of what had happened over recent months but there was no time to say all he wanted to. He soon realised he had been talking incessantly, driven by anxiety. It was an attempt to encapsulate everything within the one short visit.

Cynthia said a solicitor had visited her at home and would be coming to see him in a few days. That, with her presence was enough to send his optimism soaring. Things were moving faster than he could have expected. He was even beginning to feel confident that he would be bailed soon. Everything seemed to be working in his favour at last. He made up his mind that whatever the outcome, he would serve his sentence and then put the whole experience behind him. Things had suddenly changed for the better. He was even confident that if he got a custodial sentence, it would be lenient.

Sweet Man too was all smiles and reassurances during the visit. A good layman, tactical psychologist, he tried to encourage Michael to lift his spirits. There was hardly time to fill the void between them in such a short visit. He had been Michael's mentor since they first met but both knew that this was a different set of circumstances. A short visit didn't allow them to talk about anything at length. After the emotional reunion and his first outpouring, there wasn't much time to talk more and the last few minutes were spent in meaningless chit-chat. Before they realised, the visit was over.

The reunion was for Michael only tarnished by the absence of Uncle Ben. He had suffered a heart attack three weeks earlier, probably brought on by his excessive lifestyle. Thinking about Uncle Ben, Michael spent the rest of the day worrying after his visitors left. He had coped with most traumas, especially those he had recently experienced but Uncle Ben didn't have that luxury. He had pushed himself to the limit over the years, in so many ways, and now everyone feared the worst. Visiting him would be Michael's first priority if he got bail.

Two days later, the solicitor turned up. He was very early, just after breakfast. Short and slightly balding, he was wearing a crumpled suit. It looked like he had slept in it. Michael hoped he wouldn't appear in court to defend him looking like that. Appearance and articulation were important factors in a court of law. He already knew that some judges tended to treat solicitors who didn't look or play the part with a degree of contempt. The general rule was, as Sweet Man used to say, 'Don't go into a courtroom looking weak and incompetent, or too cocky either.'

When they started to discuss the case, the solicitor told him he would make an application for bail tomorrow. Despite his ragged appearance, he seemed competent, and to know what he was talking about, from a legal stand point. He even quoted cases that set precedents. As they discussed the case and strategies for dealing with it, Michael became gradually more confident in his solicitor's ability. He was more articulate than he had first imagined. The only worry was his dress sense.

Bail was duly granted forty eight hours later, after a brief court appearance. The solicitor asked for a few weeks to prepare the case for the defence and that too was granted.

Many of Michael's friends were there to give their support and he felt as if it was the best day of his life. When he left the court, celebrations followed immediately outside the courtroom and he was treated like a hero although he felt a flawed hero who had let a lot of people down, by being caught up in the whole scenario. Still, he thought to himself, *A half hero is better than no hero at all*. It was a moment to be flippant.

A Party was planned, and although this seemed premature, the party was on. All his friends wanted to fully celebrate his freedom. For now he was a free, happy man.

The first thing he did after leaving court, was to visit Uncle Ben in hospital to find him much worse than expected. *Critical but stable*. Nevertheless there was a smile on his face as he acknowledged Michael's arrival. With some effort, he raised his hand. Michael was reminded of the many times he had seen him do that with a glass in his hand to demand everyone's attention.

Although a sombre reunion, Uncle Ben would occasionally, with a spark of energy, summon the strength to raise a hint of laughter. When he tried to speak his voice was almost inaudible and it was clearly taxing him to try. Michael held his hand and comforted him. He had lived his life with exuberance and energy, rarely holding back and seldom compromising. It seemed it all caught up with him in one mad rush - his past hard working life and his age.

Before Michael left the hospital, Uncle Ben whispered in his ear that, he should go back home, bring some law and order to Jamaica, and make the island a better place to live. He then drifted off into what appeared to be sleep, or semi-consciousness and a nurse came and sat by his bedside to comfort him as the visit ended.

Sweet Man volunteered to go up to Birmingham to get information which might help Michael. He knew a great deal about life in the black communities of Toxteth, in Liverpool, of St Paul's, in Bristol, of Chapel Town in Leeds and of the Front Line in Handsworth. And he knew a lot of people.

When he returned to London, he confirmed that Danny was in jail. He had also discovered that Mr. Anastasia was one of the chief drug barons in Birmingham, supplying marijuana and other substances to the black community. With international links in Colombia, Morocco and Afghanistan, he was a linchpin in a worldwide operation with money invested in several casinos and sex joints, as well as illegal gambling clubs. No wonder the authorities were keen to get their hands on him.

Uncle Ben died from pneumonia, two weeks after Michael's visit. Sweet Man read his eulogy in church, highlighting his adventures, exploits, travels, experiences, and his final wish. Long before he had even considered departing from this world, he had left instructions to make sure white rum flowed profusely in his memory. He wanted his passing to be a celebration rather than a lamentation and had left enough money in his will so that personal friends and associates could celebrate his passing. His will was explicit. He didn't want any tears after his death, *just beers, and if anyone was feeling glum they should reach for the rum.*

Corny as that sounded to everyone around him, he had repeated it often enough for them to hear and remember.

His wishes were respected. Even Agnes and her undercover

German lover attended the funeral and reception and shed some tears as Uncle Ben was laid to rest. It was set of him truthfully that he was aware of all his own shortcomings and had had very few regrets about any of his unfulfilled dreams or his extremely chequered past; he had acknowledged his weaknesses but had never been fazed.

His final wishes were honoured and everyone had a great time celebrating his life.

CHAPTER SEVENTEEN

The solicitor's suit was in fact well pressed when they entered the court room. Many friends and admirers turned up, some fearing the worse, but hoping for the best. The British interrogator was also there, looking nonchalant.

A single charge of being in possession of a stolen car was read out. Michael waited for other charges, but none came. To his astonishment there was nothing about Pickersgill, Mr Anastasia, Danny, stolen bullion, Spandau or Colchester. For whatever reason, those were miraculously to be swept under the carpet. The interrogator whose name Michael never learned had obviously manipulated the situation and had kept his promise to help in return for Michael's future co-operation.

Michael's defence hinged on the assertion that in driving the car to Germany he had been merely a paid chauffeur. He denied knowing that the car was stolen and it seemed that not even the judge knew any details about what had taken place in Birmingham and Berlin.

The interrogator was called to the stand and gave a name that Michael simply did not believe was the man's own. He told the judge that Michael was arrested in Berlin on suspicion of having stolen property in his possession and made it clear there was no evidence to suggest Michael was anything but a paid driver.

The case was dismissed. It was as if everything had been pre-arranged and the decision a foregone conclusion. After the hearing, the interrogator shook his hand, wished him good luck and promised he would keep in touch.

Although he walked away from court a free man, there was only one thing on Michael's mind. He wanted to forget his past, painful experiences and start making plans to leave for Jamaica. He had no intentions of keeping in contact with anyone from recent years except close friends. The only other person he intended to contact was Ingrid and then he would be on his way to Jamaica, as soon as possible. Knowledge of his stays in Spandau, Colchester, and Brixton prisons was now widespread among friends, associates, admirers and critics so he didn't want to become too complacent. Danny, Mr Anastasia and Pickersgill had many friends. Who knew what might happen in the future if he gave evidence against them? He had promised the interrogator that he would help him in future but if he wasn't available he couldn't help. *Would he get police protection if he turned up as a witness for the prosecution?* He wasn't relying on that. He thought the best decision he could make was to leave England as soon as possible. His dream now was to marry Cynthia and practise law in Jamaica. It was time to move on.

Cynthia was still living with Hyacinth and Michael moved in with them after the court hearing. He spent the next few weeks consolidating his relationship with Cynthia and making plans to go home. He didn't discuss any details about Ingrid or any in-depth explanation about what happened in Berlin. He just wanted to put the whole experience behind him and start all over again.

A few weeks after the court hearing, he tried phoning Ingrid but there was no answer. The phone just kept ringing. It was the same when he tried again. It was Michael's one frustration that he wanted to hear her voice - to make sure she was OK and to thank her for all she had done for him – but couldn't. Part of him would have liked to arrange a meeting before he left for Jamaica but he had no idea how that could happen if he couldn't even contact her because going back to Berlin was certainly not an option.

The notion was dismissed. He wasn't prepared to do anything that might damage his relationship with Cynthia but he continued to phone her flat occasionally. The last time he telephoned, a woman answered the phone and said, 'Fraulein Muller doesn't live here anymore.'

He slowly hung up the phone, wondering whether he would ever see or hear from Ingrid again. It seemed she had decided to move. Her frightening experience at the hands of Pickersgill and Wolfgang, the car chase that nearly cost their lives, and being held in custody by the German police, had been too much for her. Perhaps what had been even more painful emotionally for her was Cynthia's existence as the main person in Michael's life. During the brief time they spent together in Berlin, there was a growing attachment, which in her eyes might have developed into something more permanent. But that was never going to happen. Michael was intensely grateful for the help she had given him and the time they had spent together and wished he could find some way of repaying her but that seemed impossible now. He never tried to contact her again.

Michael and Cynthia were now focussed on flying back to Jamaica for good. There was a strong sense of urgency as they started preparing for the flight home. They kept everything a secret and a week before they left, they had a surprise farewell party at Hyacinth's place inviting all their friends. Manto was solemn because of Uncle Ben's absence but he toasted Uncle Ben's several times during the evening, honouring his wishes that they should let the white rum flow.

Michael was treated like a local celebrity. Everyone at the party wanted to know what it was like in Spandau and whether he had met Rudolf Hess. He wasn't too keen to talk about those experiences. They were still too fresh in his mind. All he wanted to do was to abandon bitter memories. He was looking forward to a Caribbean sun beating down on his back and the taste of warm tropical air. He didn't want to reflect on the circumstance that nearly took his freedom and breath away.

Apart from Sweet Man, Manto, Linton, and a few other close friends, no one else at the party had had prior knowledge of their imminent departure. When Michael announced that he was planning to go back to Jamaica in a few days, they all wished him well. A few expressed mixed feelings and regrets but most thought he was doing the right thing after what had happened to him over the past few months.

Towards the end of the party Michael gave them even more surprising news. He announced that he and Cynthia would be getting married.

Thanks to Sweet Man Michael was no longer under the impression that being married and having his own business would be a bed of roses. Jamaica would be a different place to the one he had left all those years ago. Still, alcohol, music, laughter and good companionship had pushed him to abandon any fears he might have about the future.

Towards the end, people drifted home after saying their parting goodbyes and giving the happy couple their best wishes. Those left behind in the living room, were in pensive mood, induced in large part by an excess of the demon drink. It became a time to reflect on many things, including Uncle Ben's life. They shared the moments of distant and recent history that shaped their lives; determine their predicaments and reflected on their lives and experiences.

For Michael to be part of this situation was educational and uplifting. Some people might have expected, before he returned to Jamaica, to hear him delve into his past, with flare and heroism. That would have been what Uncle Ben would have done if he was alive. He would have embellished and added humour and excitement to the story he would tell, until the truthful origins were overshadowed by his myth-making. Michael was different. He didn't want to dwell on the idea of what might have been. He didn't even want to talk about how he had survived psychologically.

Sweet Man made a final toast and everyone drank and shared their laughter in the way Uncle Ben would have wanted.

It was an emotional farewell affair and all there wished Michael and Cynthia a safe journey, a happy marriage and a successful future.

CHAPTER EIGHTEEN

Sweet Man drove them to Heathrow airport on a misty morning. It reminded Michael of the first day he had landed in England, when the weather was such a complete contrast to what he had left behind in Jamaica. He had adapted over the years but now he was moving away from the mist into sunlight, feeling a new beginning; looking forward to going back home but it wasn't just a sense of wanting to escape the past, although that was also part of his thinking. It was more an urgent desire to leap into the future. He was now in a hurry and had no time to entertain doubts.

As they drove towards the airport, there were moments of silence, in between conversation. Those moments felt natural when people were parting, perhaps not to meet for a long time, or ever again. There were unspoken, quiet moments of sadness that could only be expressed in silence. Michael was happy to be leaving but sad because he knew in his heart that this was a one-way flight. He would never again see the friends he had left behind - unless they visited Jamaica. He was however extremely happy to be distancing himself from the possibility of having to become a witness for the prosecution. That was one way of avoiding retribution.

Flying across the Atlantic Ocean for hours, on his way to Jamaica, was not a concern. The journey from Germany to England had been his second flight and he was learning to submit to the necessity of being thirty thousand feet up in the air and to relax. He had concluded that what would happen, would happen. *Murphy's Law*, if you like. He surrendered his fate to whatever deity elected to protect him as soon as he boarded the plane.

The final moments with Sweet Man, before boarding the plane had ended in a three-way embraced and Michael's promise to write.

Sweet Man's final farewell words were: 'Safe travel, remember who you are and give my love to Jamaica. Keep cool.'

The routine leading to take-off was entirely normal. Soon the plane taxied along the slightly misty runway and the lift off was effortless as the plane climbed steeply away. As he braced himself, England and Berlin seemed suddenly far away. The past was already becoming a distant memory although he this moment wasn't a dream, because Cynthia was sitting next to him. They unfastened their seatbelts and smiled at each other. For that brief moment, no words were necessary. It was time to stop looking back.

The plane approached Montego Bay airport in bright sunshine and landed with the same ease with which it had taken off. They both breathed a sigh of relief, almost in unison as the plane came to a standstill. Passengers cheered the pilot and everyone reached for their hand luggage. As the door opened and they began to disembark, a rush of warm air surrounded them. It triggered smiles, a feeling of satisfaction and happiness.

A brief shower of rain must have fallen just before landing and the baked earth was drying out. For Michael, the smell of rain on parched earth was a childhood memory, long forgotten. It put him in the best possible mood.

As he walked towards the arrival lounge, filled with people with unpainted smiles, he thought about the contrast with Heathrow. He was now among a sea of grinning faces, the faces that gave Jamaica its distinctiveness.

'Welcome to Jamaica! Are you coming back to stay or are you on holiday?' asked the female customs officer, a wide smile on her face. It was as if they were long last relatives and she was welcoming them home. For Michael, her Jamaican accent was also refreshing to hear.

'We're here to stay. Yea, back for good,' they answered, almost in unison.

'Welcome home.' She quickly riffled through their passports and waved them on.

From that moment on Michael started readjusting to Jamaican mood and culture. To come back to an environment he had left all those years, would have been a problem for many people but for Michael, the adjustment was easy. Before he left Jamaica he was fully socialised, so adapting held no fears for him. He was British, West Indian, but Jamaican first, and that hadn't changed despite the years spent in England.

They ended up staying with relatives for several months, while they made plans to do the things they had talked about in England. Eventually, they moved to Kingston, Cynthia got a senior post at the hospital and Michael opened his law business. Originally, he planned to call the business: *The Wright Practice* but abandoned that idea for obvious reasons. Instead he changed his surname by deed poll and used that on his letterhead. He never discusses his past experiences with anyone and doesn't intend to. When anyone wants to know his background he tells them that he met Cynthia in England when they were students.

Michel kept his promise to Sweet Man that he would write to him regularly but there was no news to be had about Danny, or Mr. Anastasia. The past was erased to the point where their fate ceased to hold any interest to him. Now that they were a world apart and he was with Cynthia, they had ceased to matter.

Michael's mother returned from Canada after a few more years, pleased to find her son a happily married and successful businessman. She couldn't help being overtly proud of her son's achievements and invited all her friends and extended family to yet another celebratory

The party was in full swing when his mother decided she would make a little speech about how proud she was of her son and his wife. 'I am very proud of my son and his beautiful wife, Cynthia. As you know, they were both been studying in England and are fully qualified. They are a credit to Jamaica. Michael is a good boy. He's behaved flawlessly all his life and never got into trouble of any kind. He doesn't mix with undesirables or criminals, nor does he fall foul of the law. That's why he is such a successful lawyer.'

The crowd applauded with sincerity. Michael and Cynthia glanced at each other. He was hoping his mother wouldn't ask him to confirm what she had just said. If she did, he would never contradict her, as a matter of respect. He would prefer to tell his lies as a lawyer.

Printed in Great Britain
by Amazon